ALL THE
TOMORROWS

•

FRANCES ENGLE
WILSON

AVALON BOOKS
THOMAS BOUREGY AND COMPANY, INC.
401 LAFAYETTE STREET
NEW YORK, NEW YORK 10003

PRINTED IN THE UNITED STATES OF AMERICA
ON ACID-FREE PAPER
BY HADDON CRAFTSMEN, SCRANTON, PENNSYLVANIA

To Renee, a talented writer and a dear daughter-in-law.

And in memory of Gladys, Isabelle, and Thyrza,
who, in their own different ways, let me see the magic of
live theater.

For all the tomorrows
Time without end,
There's love to share
There're dreams to spend.

F.E.W.

Chapter One

It was a cold, icy January morning. Tori awakened to the sound of sleet pattering against the window panes accompanied by the low moan of the wind. Reaching down to the end of her bed for her robe, she was thrusting her arms into its warm fleecy sleeves when her phone started ringing. Her apartment was a modest two-room efficiency, and the telephone sat on the bar counter that acted as a room divider between the kitchen and living area. The bell jangled a second and a third time before Tori located her terry scuffs and padded out of the bedroom to grab up the receiver.

"Thank goodness you're there Tori. Because I've got something really big for you. Big like in prime grade, Broadway theater." The sharp staccato voice of Tori's agent battered her ear with much the same in-

1

tensity as the ice pellets hitting the window glass. ''Now listen carefully. You get your talented self to the Empire Theater at ten-thirty this morning. I mean ten-thirty sharp, you hear me.''

''Loud and clear, Jayson. You're practically yelling. What's this all about anyway?''

''You're big chance, honey. That's what it's about. I've set up an audition for you with none other than Maxwell Branton. How does that grab you?'' Jayson paused then, as if he anticipated her excited reaction to what he'd done for her.

''Is this on the level? Are you really serious?'' Tori's voice rose in disbelief.

''Would I kid with a client of mine about a chance at a part in a play Max Branton is directing.'' His voice slowed and mellowed. ''I beat my gums promoting you for this one, Tori. Even delivered your photograph and resume to Ol' Max myself. You'd better know it's on the level!''

''Oh, Ja—Jayson. That's great. I—I mean it's—it's tremendous,'' she stammered, trembling all over both from her excitement and the cold apartment. ''But his current play has been running for over a year now. What's the audition for?''

''It's for the secondary lead in *Rowena's Daughter*.''

Puzzled, Tori frowned. ''Melissa Gallagher plays that part. I saw her in it only three months ago. Surely, she's not leaving the cast.''

"Yeah, she has to. Seems she's pregnant and has developed some problems. Her doctor says there's too great a risk for her to stay with the play until the end of the present season. The word went out four days ago that Branton has to get a new actress in the part by the first of next week." Jayson cleared his throat emphatically. "So get moving, Tori," he ordered. "By no means be late for this. The wonder man, Branton, is a stickler for time. And there's a real blizzard outside too, so you could have a devil of a time getting a cab." Jayson pelted her ear again with this final barrage of words, clearly indicating that as her theatrical agent he'd done everything he could—the rest was up to her.

Jayson Klein had exaggerated the severity of the weather just as he did most things, Tori thought as she paid the cab driver later that morning. It had stopped snowing by now, and a watery sun was trying to penetrate the swollen sky, with meager success. She clutched her coat around her and headed for the theater entrance.

Tori had planned carefully for this audition. For the opportunity to try out before a director like Max Branton rarely occurred to an actress with only off-Broadway roles to her credit. Even though Tori had recently finished a moderately successful run in an off-Broadway show—in which one drama critic had called her a "new talent worth watching"—she doubted Max Branton had seen the play or read the critic's review.

Intending to have everything possible working to her advantage, Tori had dressed in a tailored, green wool suit that complemented her slim figure and harmonized with her emerald green eyes. With the suit she wore black leather boots. Tori had long slender legs, finely turned ankles and pretty arched feet. In boots, brogues or high heels she walked with grace. In some cases on stage she moved so beautifully and elegantly that a theater critic had said she had harmony of body movement that was to the eye like symphony music was to the ear. Recalling that now bolstered her self confidence as she walked quickly along the theater aisle.

The much trod aisle carpet was worn thin, and did not totally muffle the tap of her boot heels. Realizing this, Tori slowed her steps, and midway down she slipped into an aisle seat, three rows behind where two men and a woman sat observing and listening to a young, redheaded actress reading lines. It was apparent that the attractive ingenue was here for the same reason as Tori, to audition for the roll of the misfit girl in *Rowena's Daughter*.

''Nicely done, Carol. Good reading.'' One of the two men jumped to his feet and strode forward. Even from the back, Tori recognized that the man was Maxwell Branton. Though she'd never actually met him, she had seen him several times. Once at the Russian

Tearoom, he'd been in one of the red leather booths adjacent to where she and her agent were having lunch with an advertising executive who was using Tori in a television commercial.

Tori's interested gaze followed the director's broad shoulders as he approached the stage. She took notice of his splendid dark head set proudly on his strong neck. Max Branton was certainly a man who carried himself with self-assurance. And well he might, for at thirty-two he had written and directed three major box-office successes. As a playwright he had been compared to Harold Pinter and Tennessee Williams; as a director, even the legendary actress Corinne Hayes, who played the lead in each of his three Broadway plays, was quoted as saying he made her act better than she knew how to.

Now as Max leaped onto the stage to talk with the actress who had just finished her audition, the footlights revealed his unlined face to be well-featured, his ears flat against his head, and his black hair thick and smooth, coming down at the back to meet the shining edge of his collar. He had a strong Roman nose, and a wide mouth that revealed even, white teeth as he smiled approvingly at the actress before him. Obviously he was taken with this girl's audition. Had he already made up his mind to offer her the coveted part in his play? If so, Tori's reading would be anti-climactic. More than likely he would only give her token time and attention.

Angry at herself for getting in such a state, Tori deliberately looked away from the stage and studied the man and woman who sat a few rows in front of her. She was wondering who they might be, and if they were involved in some way with the production of *Rowena's Daughter.*

As if the woman felt Tori's eyes on her back, she shifted around in her seat, glancing over her shoulder, and acknowledged Tori with a nod and a slender, momentary smile.

Tori's mouth flew open in a gasp of surprise. The woman was Corinne Hayes, the star of Branton's play and the reigning first lady of the New York stage. Why would Corinne Hayes be spending time at the theater watching these auditions? Was Max Branton going to let her have something to say about the actress chosen to take Melissa Gallagher's place? And the man sitting beside Corinne, Tori wondered who he might be. Was he someone in the play? She could only see the back of his head, so she wasn't able to tell much about him. For some reason, however, she sensed that he was here because of Corinne, and more than likely he was not in the cast of *Rowena's Daughter.*

Before she had time to speculate further, she heard her name being called.

"I'm ready for Miss Trent. Is she here?"

Tori jumped up from her seat. "I'm here, Mr. Branton," she answered, stepping quickly out into the aisle.

"Good." He shot his shirt cuff up his wrist, glancing at his watch. "And I see you're prompt. I like that." He waved her forward, indicating that he wished her to join him on stage. "Jayson Klein told me you were an actress with a fine sense of timing. Seems he's right so far." The director smiled as if pleased both with her and his own wit.

Tori smiled back and ran lightly up the steps onto the stage. Her boot heels made a crisp tapping sound as she walked across the bare wooden platform to meet him center stage.

Max appraised her with discerning eyes that were wide-set beneath his dark eyebrows. "You move well," he said, his vibrant voice suddenly subdued to a quiet conversational tone. "Anybody ever tell you that?"

His unexpected compliment surprised her, causing her to frown and look at him obliquely for a second. "Yes," she answered. "Once." She gave a faint shrug.

"Who?" He asked with a slow smile, his gaze remaining on her face.

"It was one of the play reviewers. He wrote that I had harmony of movement." She arched her head just enough to look up at him. "Something or other like that," she said with a modest smile.

"He was right—you do, Miss Trent." He studied her a fraction of a second more before lifting the yellow writing pad he held to look at what he had written on it. "I see here that your name is Tori. So tell me Tori. Are you familiar with the plot of *Rowena's Daughter?*"

She nodded. "I saw it a number of months ago. It's an absorbing play and marvelously acted."

"Yes, it is. I intend to see that it remains that way." He was all business now, and he pushed one hand through the front of his hair, smoothing it back from his forehead. "So what d'you say we hear you read."

He walked over and picked up the script the other actress had left on a folding chair, which was the only prop on the otherwise barren stage. Handing the playbook to Tori, he said. "Take a few minutes to look at the first scene in act two. Then when you're ready you can begin." Offering these brief instructions, Max strode off the stage, returning to his seat beside Corinne Hayes.

Tori's attention became immediately riveted to the script she gripped tensely in her hand. Riffling the pages, she located the part the director had asked for. Her green eyes avidly searched out the daughter's lines in a gripping scene of betrayed trust. Max Branton had told her to take a few minutes, and she sensed a *few* was precisely what he expected her to require. Fortunately she was adept at sight reading a role. She took as long as she dared to evaluate the emotional power in the specific scene and determine how she could make the most of it. Then looking out first at the empty seats in the dimly lit area, she took several steps down stage. It was absurd, but for an odd moment she was conscious of the somewhat dusty and stale smells that hovered in the scantily heated theater. She let her eyes briefly touch on the faces of the three people who were sitting out there in the void watching her, then simply began reading in a soft, yet crystal-clear voice.

In the following minutes as the complex scene unfolded, Tori ran a full gamut of emotions. After all she was an ambitious actress, and she had worked tirelessly through four years of study to develop the skills of her craft. She brought all she had to this audition, fully aware that this was the greatest opportunity she had yet been offered. When she finished the long scene, she clutched the playbook tight to her breast, waiting, head slightly bowed, for Max Branton to comment.

Max contemplated her for a thoughtful moment, remaining seated, but leaning forward his chin resting on the back of his hand. ''Very well done,'' he said finally, stressing each of his words equally. He nodded his head toward her as he spoke, yet he didn't move from his seat. Rather, he leaned back and turned to Corinne Hayes to engage her in a low-voiced discussion.

Tori stood rooted to her spot on stage, uncertain of what the director expected of her, if indeed he wished anything further. Maybe he intended to dismiss her with only those three words. She pressed her lips to-

gether as tension set off a chain reaction of all the
nerves in her body. He had sounded positive when
he'd said she'd done the scene very well. Why didn't
he say something more? And what were he and the
star of his play talking about?

Tori's anxieties mounted. Her eyes felt hot and
parched just as if she'd been looking up at the sun on
a torrid July day. She closed her eyes, squeezing them
tightly shut to force a relieving film of moisture over
them. When she opened her eyes and looked out front
again, she was surprised to see Max stepping out in
the aisle to allow Corinne to pass in front of him.

"Corinne is coming to join you, Tori," he announced. "The two of you will run through a bit in
the third act." He slipped into his seat again, then
called out as an afterthought. "Maybe you two actresses haven't met. Tori Trent meet our play's superlative leading lady, Corinne Hayes." He stretched his
arms out, palms upward, indicating each of them.

Tori's heart was pounding fast and hard, so hard, in
fact, that the script she had pressed against her breast
vibrated in her hands. Corinne walked toward her with
quick light steps, a small but regal figure in a decep-
tively simple, black wool dress. Her dark auburn hair
was parted in the center and framed her oval face that
had   perfectly   balanced   features   and   an   illusion
of ageless beauty. Tori gazed in awe at the celebrated
actress, recalling things she'd read and heard about
her. As a Broadway personality, Corinne Hayes had

been featured in articles in all the leading women's magazines, and even had her twenty-year or more theater career profiled in *The New Yorker*. Why, while Tori was still in drama school Corinne's picture had been on the cover of *Time*. In all that Tori had read about her, however, they had never revealed how old she was. Surely she had to be close to fifty, but her age was a well-kept secret, as was practically everything else about her. The public was told everything about this renowned actress that was unimportant, very little that truly mattered.

As Corinne joined her at close range Tori detected a certain coarseness in her skin because it had known too much stage makeup. "You were splendid," Corinne whispered, her gleaming amber eyes studying Tori with interest. "Just let me have the playbook," she flashed Tori a warm, encouraging smile. "I'll find the scene that we'll run through together." She extended a slender-fingered hand which surprisingly was unadorned. The actress had such expressive hands that it struck Tori as unusual that Corinne didn't wear a ring or two to dramatize each graceful gesture. As the older actress leafed through the script, Tori continued to study her in fascination. Not only did she not wear rings, she wore no jewelry with her chic black dress except for three twisted strands of freshwater pearls.

Corinne began the scene in her marvelous, deep-toned voice. Tori took her cue as to tempo and mood from the star. The dialogue flowed smoothly and the short scene played well.

The second they finished, Max clapped his hands in quick applause. "Bravo," he called out to them. "You two are effective together."

"Yes, we are," Corinne agreed, giving Tori a conspiratorial smile accompanied by a self-satisfied arching of her well-shaped brows.

"As always, Corinne, you're invaluable to me." Max silenced her before she could elaborate with her own evaluation of Tori's audition. "Thanks for coming down this morning, and now I won't detain you and Griff any longer." He dismissed her with a charm-laden smile.

At this, the man beside Max stood up and gathered Corinne's dark mink coat from the seat where the actress had left it. He was a tall, distinguished-looking man with iron gray hair and a lean, somewhat severe face. It was an attractive face nonetheless, clean-lined, keen and intelligent. He walked toward the stage to meet Corinne and draped the fur around her shoulders, wasting no time in escorting her from the theater.

Max now focused his full attention on Tori. "Come down and sit with me," he ordered, his authoritative voice sounding loud as it echoed in the empty theater. "I've several things to discuss with you."

Tori hesitated, wondering what she should do with the script: take it with her, or leave it on the folding chair as the actress before her had done. Max must have sensed her predicament, for when she started over to the chair with it he called out to her. "Bring the playbook with you."

She nodded and hurried from the stage. Nervous chills trembled through her as she experienced conflicting feelings of expectancy and uncertainty. Would he choose her for the part? He did seem pleased with her audition. Too, Corinne had made her approval obvious. Things appeared to be in her favor.

Max lowered the aisle seat as she came to him, indicating that was where he wanted her to sit. Turning sideways he looked at her, his eyes blue as open water and quite disconcerting in the steadiness of their gaze. "I like the tonal quality of your voice. It balances nicely with Corinne's. I particularly noticed that. It's good—also pleasing." He appraised her with that penetrating look of his. Tori pressed her lips together and said nothing.

"Your voice is slightly higher pitched which gives youthful contrast to the mature mellowness of Corinne's. Exactly right for the mother—daughter. . . . " He hesitated and gestured with his hands as if he were juggling two objects of equal weight. "What I'm saying is that you project the illusion I want for *Rowena's Daughter.*" Max smiled at her and took her hand, shaking it firmly. "Welcome to our cast Tori."

Filled with elation Tori's eyes mirrored her excitement. "Oh, this is wonderful. Thank you." She gave a happy sigh. "You must know how much this means to me. I—I don't know what else to say—but thank you, Mr. Branton. Thank you so much.'' Joy sounded through each word she uttered.

"One thank you is quite enough Tori," he said with an amused smile and a shrug. "And I'll wager when you get to know me and discover how good I expect you to be in my play, you may not even say that."

"Yes, I will," she answered. "I'm grateful for the opportunity you're giving me and I'll give it everything I've got. I promise you that, Mr. Branton."

"Okay." He held out his hand to silence her. "Let's get a few things settled. First off, call me Max. What we respect in the theater is talent, not titles. People who work with me call each other by their names. I want it that way. And along with that I can't abide the affectation of actors and actresses who call everyone darling." Max's lip curled in repugnance. "If I call someone darling it is because they are dear to me and loved, not because they are acting in my production." He frowned suddenly and rubbed his hand across his chin. "Say, I sure got off on a tangent there, and I'll be darned if I know why." He gave a disparaging laugh. "What I intended to do was list my immediate expectations of you. I want you to memorize all your lines by tomorrow and report here at two o'clock for rehearsal. When you've done that you'll see Maida who's in charge of wardrobe for costume fittings." He leaned toward her, his eyes fixed on hers. "You'll play the Saturday matinee for me Tori," he said, taking her hand in his warm grasp once again. "And you'll give me a first-rate performance, I know."

Her eyes widened and she returned his steady gaze, at the same time experiencing the vital charisma that sprang from his compelling personality. What was it about him that was affecting her so? True, he projected a curious combination of authority and charming savoir-faire, and more than that, an animal magnetism that was magical. That was no reason for her to act like a mesmerized ingenue however. She swallowed hard, struggling to regain some professional composure. "I'll be ready for that Saturday performance. You can count on it." Tori felt amazed that her voice sounded even and did not reveal how thrown off balance she was feeling. Easing her hand from his grasp, she edged out of her seat. "I expect I'd best take the script and get home and start memorizing lines." A tremulous smile touched her mouth briefly, then vanished.

"Good idea," Max replied as Tori rose to her feet. He stood up then too, and standing next to her eyed her again curiously. "Tell me something, Tori." His dark brows lowered in a frown. "I've never met you before today have I?"

She shook her head. "No."

"I know you though. It's odd, but I honestly feel I know you." He searched her face with questioning eyes. "Must have been in a play, I guess." He shrugged. "A character in a play must have been like you—young, ambitious, and moving with a grace that's beautiful to watch. Reality and illusion do get confused in the world of theater I've discovered.'' He smiled and stepped away from her to indicate she was free to go.

Tori felt Max's eyes follow her as she picked up her coat and walked back up the aisle. It was incredulous, but Max had voiced the same feelings she had been aware of. A moment ago when he had first taken her hand and welcomed her to the cast of *Rowena's Daughter,* she too had been shaken with an astonishing feeling of recognition. Somehow—some way—she felt she knew this man. It was as if some part of her had always known him.

Chapter Two

Tori reached the lobby just as the outside door swung open admitting a blast of cold air. A tall brunette covered from her ankles to her chin in a scarlet red wool coat dashed inside. She wore no hat atop her long dark hair, only a pair of white angora ear muffs which she pulled off as she caught sight of Tori.

"Hi there," she murmured breathlessly. "Is Max still around?"

"Yes." Tori nodded. "I just left him inside."

The young woman glanced at the clock in the lobby. "Eleven thirty-five," she moaned. "I blew it. I'll bet the auditions are over, aren't they?"

Tori nodded. "I was the last one."

"Well, how's his mood?" She slanted her blue-gray eyes questioningly. "Good or bad?"

17

Tori found this an odd question, but she smiled and answered. "I'd say good. However, this is the first time I've auditioned for him. He seemed pretty great to me. Say," Tori studied the other woman's face. "Weren't you in Max Branton's last play?"

"Yeah, I played the younger sister in *Tattered Ribbons.* I'm Monica Wells. And you're. . . . "

"Tori Trent." They exchanged smiles.

"Max is wonderful, but he hates it when you're late. Which I usually am," Monica said with a self-deprecating grimace. "So I'm glad if you left him in a favorable frame of mind. Thanks for that." She flipped her hand in a parting salute and hurried off to find Max. Tori fastened her coat against the cold and headed outside to flag down a taxi.

An uneasy thought nagged at the corner of her mind. It would seem that Monica Wells had intended to audition for the role in *Rowena's Daughter,* but missed out by coming to the theater so late. Tori couldn't help but wonder what would have happened if Monica had made the auditions on time. Since she'd appeared in one of Max Branton's plays before, wouldn't that have given her an edge? Besides she was a more experienced actress and striking to look at with that raven hair and alabaster skin.

Tori shook her head to clear away such worrisome ideas. After all, Max Branton had given the role to her. That was what was important. Thank goodness Jayson had warned her about getting to the audition on time. She smiled inwardly then, her earlier excitement returning. It certainly pays to listen to what your agent tells you. She thanked her lucky stars she'd done that.

Tori spent the next two afternoons at the theater, becoming familiar with the set for *Rowena's Daughter,* going through the various bits of stage business that her part called for, and learning from which spots to make her entrances and exits. Max coached her through her major scenes, getting her ready for the full cast rehearsal scheduled for later in the week.

"I warned you I was a hard taskmaster," he told her, after he'd asked her to repeat a particular scene for the third time. "I think you've earned a short break now though." He motioned her into the wings. "I've got a coffee maker in the office and I'll reward your efforts by letting you share a box of chocolate cookies. Come with me." He smiled, waiting for her to join him.

Apparently there was nobody about, not even the custodian. They were surrounded by the hollow kind of silence that pervades an empty theater. Tori could smell that peculiar moldy smell indigenous to every backstage. It was a strange odor compounded of dry dust, musty mildew, the resinous fumes emanating from the varnished sets, plus the ever-present grease-paint, hair spray and stale cigarette smoke. Tori welcomed these pervasive smells of a New York theater. To her it was actually intoxicating.

A naked drop light swung above them, causing eerie

shadows in the dim hallway. Max hesitated at the open office door, reaching inside to snap on the lights. Either all but one of the bulbs in the round glass ceiling fixture were burned out, or the glass cover was filled with dust and grime. At any rate it only produced a minimum of murky light.

"You take the chair behind the desk," Max suggested. "It has a cushioned pad which makes it the only halfway comfortable seat I can offer." He stepped aside to let her enter, directing her to the flat-topped, oak desk that took up a third of the box-shaped room. On the adjacent wall stood two metal file cabinets. A Silex coffee maker occupied the top of one cabinet and beside it was a short stack of styrofoam cups. "I've got sweetener and powdered creamer if you like it."

"I prefer it black."

"Good. Me too." He opened the top drawer of the second cabinet, took out a box of cookies and slid the box across the desk toward her. Then he poured two cups of coffee and as soon as he'd set them on the desk he grabbed up a straight chair, pulling it up so he could sit by the desk facing her.

"Oh good! These are Oreos. My favorites." Tori removed two of the cream filled chocolate cookies from the package then turned the open box where Max could reach it.

"We both like coffee black and Oreos. Gives us

something more in common than merely acting and the theater.''

''Not if you're one of those who separate the cookies and lick the filling,'' she said, teasing him because he'd started to twist his Oreo apart.

At her words Max immediately pressed it together again. ''Surely you don't think I'd do anything as childish as that.'' He gave her a sheepish grin. ''I was just checking to see if the cookies are still fresh and the centers creamy.''

''Of course you were,'' she commented primly.

''And what's your view on dunking?'' He asked with a straight face.

''I'm definitely for that.'' She dipped part of her cookie into her coffee to emphasize her statement. ''Now I think you and I've covered the Oreo question rather thoroughly, don't you.'' Her laughing eyes mocked him.

His eyes now were brimming with amusement. ''I'd say we've touched all aspects of the subject, and at the same time gotten your mind off of acting for a minute. That's exactly what I wanted to do,'' he said with satisfaction.

''I was feeling a bit uptight about that last scene.'' Tori took a drink of her coffee.

''You needn't have. Trust me. It will all come together just fine tomorrow when you rehearse it with Corinne,'' he reassured her. ''Now relax and finish your coffee. Then we'll run through the last act and we can quit for today.''

Max was right. With Tori's first rehearsal with the full cast she felt the melding process begin for her. After the first three performances she had blended into her role so well, that unless they'd been told, no one in the audience would believe that she hadn't played the part from the beginning.

In the weeks that followed, more things than just the play clicked into place. From the onset there had been a kind of immediate awareness between Tori and Max. Tori did not think about what was happening between them, but merely felt it, experiencing the chemistry which was emotionally drawing them together.

During January and the first few weeks in February, Tori saw Max only at the theater where they were usually surrounded by members of the cast. The occasional few moments that she and Max talked together back stage, before or after a performance, there were stagehands shifting scenery nearby. Because of this their conversations were neither private nor intimate. Yet strangely they were both. Beneath their casual words, or exchange of light banter, Tori felt a note of sensuality. More than once she found his eyes resting steadily on her, and felt the warm caress in his look. It went no further than that however.

After a while, Tori convinced herself that the attraction she felt toward him was one-sided. His interest in her was nothing more than any mild flirtation a director might have with a new actress in one of his plays.

A short time later something happened that caused Tori to wonder if Monica Wells might be romantically involved with Max. On a week night Corinne and Tori happened to arrive at the theater at the same time. The two of them were talking as they walked down the hall to their dressing rooms when Monica came dashing toward them.

''Did Max come in with either of you?'' she asked, looking first at Corinne then acknowledging Tori with a quick nod.

''No, he didn't,'' Corinne answered.

''Well I can't imagine where he could be. I've been trying to track him down for thirty minutes and I can't find him. I thought he was always at the theater by this time of the evening. It's so important that I talk to him right away. Where on earth is he?'' Her voice spiraled and she made dramatic gestures, flinging out both hands.

''If you'll calm down for a second I can tell you,'' Corinne said with an indulgent smile at the agitated actress. ''He and Robin were going to some special event at her school.''

Monica didn't try to hide her annoyance. ''Oh, Max is obsessed with that child. Talk about the doting father. He created the role.''

Corinne's eyes shimmered with anger. "Seeing to the needs of a motherless child is hardly obsessive behavior, Monica. Max is a responsible, loving parent, that's all. Robin simply takes priority over everything else in his life. You'd do well to remember that." The older actress's voice was quiet, yet held an undertone of cold contempt. "Now you can wait for him if you like, but I seriously doubt he'll get here before curtain time." Corinne turned her back on the sullen younger actress and wagged her finger to Tori. "Come on Tori, you and I have to get into makeup and ready for tonight's performance."

Tori had listened to the charged exchange between Corinne and Monica, a look of surprised bemusement on her face. Now as she walked beside Corinne toward their dressing rooms she was thinking of so many questions she was dying to ask. "I—I had no idea that Max had a child."

"Well he does, and she's just a great little girl."

"Does she look like Max?" Tori asked curiously.

Corinne's warm smile curved her lips and lit her eyes. "She looks like Robin, cornflower blue eyes, shiny long auburn hair and a pert little face. To go with that she's full of spunk and as strong-willed as her father."

"Sounds like you know her pretty well."

"I should. I've known her all her life. She's my godchild," Corinne said, a quiver of emotion in her beautifully modulated voice.

Tori looked surprised. "Oh, if you're her god-mother then I guess you were a close friend of Robin's mother. What happened to her?"

Corinne's expression darkened. "Janet died nearly two years ago." She shook her head sadly. "It was such a tragedy," she said, with a sigh filled with re-gret. She hesitated and for a moment Tori thought Cor-inne was going to tell her what had happened to Max's wife. The next instant, however, it seemed to Tori that Corinne's face closed as if she were guarding a secret. "I know it would upset Max terribly if he thought I talked about his family. After all his private life is his own and must never be a subject for backstage gos-sip." With these final words Corinne turned her back on Tori, walking immediately into her dressing room and closing the door firmly behind her.

Tori stared after Corinne feeling uncomfortable, even chastised by her words and attitude. Had she meant to reprimand Tori because she'd asked ques-tions concerning Max's family? Or did she only mean to caution her, keep her from discussing anything she'd discovered tonight with other members of the cast? With a shrug she pushed these bothersome thoughts aside. She had a performance to do tonight and it behooved her to put on her stage makeup and get into costume for the first act without any more delays.

*   *   *

It was less than two weeks later when Max asked Tori to go to supper with him following a Saturday evening performance. He extended his invitation between the second and third acts, stopping her back stage as she was hurrying to change for the final scene.

"If you don't have other plans, I'd like to take you out to eat after the play tonight." He caught hold of her arm to detain her, and leaned his face close to hers, speaking quietly as if he didn't want to be overheard.

"I don't have any plans, and I'd really like that," she responded, matching his subdued tone.

He smiled. "Great, it's a date." He let his hand slide caressingly down her arm before reluctantly letting her go.

Max took her to a place in the Village, the Wine Cellar, which occupied the first two floors of a former town house that was vaguely Tudor in style with wooden beams criss-crossing stucco. Inside the look was rough brick and unpainted wooden tables. Tori was intrigued because the menu was printed with chalk on large slates strategically placed around the room. All of the dinners began with a delicious loaf of black bread. Max ordered one of the house specialties for them, which was kebabs made with steak rather than lamb and marinated with cognac and wine.

They ate and talked for an incredibly long time. It seemed extraordinary to Tori how comfortable she felt with Max away from the theater like this. There seemed something different about him tonight. He was easy, unhurried, as though he found her company delightful and he wanted to prolong their time together. She found this flattering, especially because it had taken him so long to get around to inviting her out in the first place.

They finished their meal then lingered over dessert and coffee. They were so deep in conversation that neither of them were aware the restaurant had emptied until their waiter tactfully presented Max with the check, explaining that the Wine Cellar was closing in another ten minutes.

"They're throwing us out Tori," Max said, a woebegone expression on his face.

"Well, I'm not surprised. It's probably near dawn."

"Time to see the sunrise. That could be a good sign for us," he said, a smile springing to his lips and a bit of a gleam entering his eyes.

"How's that?" Tori slanted her head quizzically.

"The sunrise marks a new day's beginning. Couldn't it mark a beginning for you and me as well?" His eyes never wavered from hers, and something inside Tori quivered like the first uncertain notes of a new melody.

"You do have a way with words, Max. And if that isn't a line from one of your plays, it should be." Smiling, she held her hand out to him. "Come on before they really do kick us out of here."

They left the restaurant and hailed down a taxi. At Tori's apartment, Max asked the driver to wait while he took her inside. At her doorway he kissed her and a lightheadedness invaded her at the feel of the warm firmness of his lips on hers.

"I'll call you tomorrow," he promised, and though he released her he did not step away. Instead, he stood there looking at her, a half smile hovering on his lips which sent a seductive warmth stealing through her. "There's a place I go for Sunday brunch. I want to take you there tomorrow."

Max left quickly then, not waiting for her to accept or decline his invitation, if indeed she could call it that. He seemed to take it for granted that she had no other plans for Sunday; that she would go wherever he chose to take her. Folding her arms across her chest she hugged herself smiling inwardly, for naturally she intended to do exactly that. At that moment she wondered if she might not always go wherever Max wanted to take her.

The hour was incredibly late. Tori hurried to get ready for bed, hoping that she could lay her head on the pillow and fall immediately to sleep. She didn't however. She was far too keyed up. The second she closed her eyes her mind began to replay the entire evening. She recalled the things she and Max had talked about. The most fascinating for her being what he'd told her about his playwriting and his early apprentice years in the theater. He had taken all manner of backstage jobs until he garnered the opportunity to work as an assistant to an older, noted director. Working with this talented man had proved an invaluable learning experience for him, for with each succeeding play more and more responsibility was delegated to Max. Their final production together the aging director placed the reins in Max's hands, and saw to it that Max was given the major credit for the play's considerable success.

Max had recounted dozens of interesting things about this director, and also of the actors and actresses who had played important roles in the three plays he had written as well as directed. All three had starred Corinne. A fact which Max said couldn't fail to make them smashing Broadway hits.

Thinking about this, she frowned because she suddenly realized that Max hadn't spoken of any person outside of the Broadway theater. It seemed strange that with all they'd talked about he had not once mentioned something about his little daughter. She couldn't help but wonder why he had not.

Chapter Three

The following day was crisp and cool as could be expected for a Sunday in mid-March. Max came for her at eleven o'clock, and they decided to walk for a while before going to Max's favorite Sunday eating place. As they started down the block Max looped her arm through his, fitting his stride to hers so they moved together in perfectly coordinated steps.

The sun, which likes to visit New York but doesn't care to live there, lay in shafts and streaks and geometrical patterns on the wide city streets. There was an electricity in the air, Manhattan electricity that never failed to energize Tori. Even on Sunday the Big Apple seemed vibrant and alive. For it had its own pulse, a special tempo that was unique and which Tori never failed to find exciting. She felt this now as she and Max walked in companionable silence, looking around at the canyon of steel and shimmering glass that was Manhattan.

"I like walking with you. You really pick your feet up and put 'em down," Max said after they'd covered several long blocks. "But this isn't a marathon, so what do you say we slow down a bit." He pressed his fingers firmly over Tori's wrist holding her back a bit.

"I was just keeping up with you," she said with a smug little laugh.

"No, I've been trying to stay in pace with you, and after a late Saturday night I'm no match for the youthful exuberance of a twenty-two-year-old on Sunday."

"Twenty-six-year-old—if you want to be accurate. But for thirty-something, I'd say you've been holding your own relatively well." She mocked him, an impish glint in her expressive eyes.

"Thirty-two—if you want to be accurate," he countered mimicking her. "Now that we've got that settled, I say we grab the next cab we see and go to brunch."

Fifteen minutes later Max was paying the cab driver at the canopied entrance to the restaurant.

"I'm glad you brought me here," Tori said enthusiastically. "I've heard the flamenco guitarist here is marvelous." She called Max's attention to the placard with the Iberian musician's picture as they entered the imposing baroque-styled room decorated with Spanish wrought iron and rich dark wood.

The maitre d' caught sight of them and immediately

rushed forward to greet Max. "Good morning, Mr. Branton. I've saved your regular table for you of course. But I don't see your charming little daughter. Isn't she going to be with you today?"

" 'Fraid not, Carlos. Robin's spending some time with her grandparents in Vermont."

Now that the maitre d' had mentioned Max's daughter, Tori grabbed at this opportunity to find out more about her. She searched her mind for a way to broach the subject without appearing unduly curious.

"You rate preferred treatment here Max. You and Robin must come here often," she said, as they picked up glasses of zesty spiced tomato juice from the base of one of the three ice sculptures decorating various areas of the sumptuous buffet table.

"Oh, once a month—sometimes twice." He lifted one shoulder in a casual shrug. "Sunday being our housekeeper's day off, Robin and I always eat out. She much prefers that to my cooking, because she claims I can't cook anything but bacon and eggs and Eggo waffles." He laughed. "And she's about right."

"Besides, what little girl wouldn't deem it a special treat to go out to Sunday dinner with her father. I know I would have." Tori's tone was wistful.

Max nodded in agreement. "It's a special time for us both. We used to pick a new place to go each week. But last October I brought Robin here on her birthday with Corinne and her friend, Griff Marland, who's at the theater with her most every night. Griff had ar-

ranged with the entertainer to come to the table and
serenade Robin. Carlos too, of course, saw to it that
Robin was treated like some kind of visiting royalty.
Robin had the typical female reaction. She's now convinced that five-star restaurants are the only way to
go.'' He made a helpless gesture with his hands.
''What does a poor ol' dad do about that?''

Tori laughed at his woeful expression. ''Just what
you are doing, I expect. Bring her here a few of the
Sundays, the rest of the time take home Chinese or
order in a pizza.''

''You know that's a good practical solution I hadn't
thought of. I'll give it a try.'' His wide mouth curved
up and a smile broke through.

Having finished their tomato juice, they started serving themselves from an array of salads, smoked
salmon and fruits and cheese. ''Let's go to the table
and eat our salads, then come back later for all the
rest,'' Max suggested.

''Good idea,'' Tori agreed. Carrying her full plate
gingerly, Tori wove her way through the dining room
to reach their table by impressive leaded glass windows. Hoping to keep Max talking about his family
she asked, ''Is it your parents or your wife's that
Robin is visiting in Vermont?''

He looked at her for a moment before he answered.
There was a sadness in his eyes as well as a tenseness
in the set of the muscles in his face and neck. ''Robin's with my parents,'' he said quietly. ''Janet's

mother and father are not living. I imagine someone at the theater has told you that my wife died two years ago too.''

Disconcerted, Tori was unsure of just what she should say. ''I'm sorry Max. All I knew was what Corinne mentioned only a few days ago. She said you were raising a daughter by yourself. My mother raised me alone so I understand some of your problems.'' She lowered her eyes to escape his questioning eyes. ''But enough about parents and daughters,'' she said, picking up her salad fork and feigning a hungry interest in her food. ''Time to eat, drink and be merry.'' She covered her embarrassment with a cliché.

As they ate a leisurely meal their conversation branched out into less personal areas. They lingered awhile longer over delicious wedges of New York cheesecake and rich aromatic coffee. After all that they decided to finish off the Sunday afternoon by taking in a highly touted foreign film.

By the time she and Max came out of the movie it was gray, dusky twilight, and there was even a hint of rain in the evening air. Max suggested going some place for supper.

Nonplussed, Tori looked at him and shook her head. ''I couldn't possibly eat another meal after that fabulous brunch. Honestly Max, I don't think you can either.''

''Maybe not steak and potatoes, but I'd consider a

sandwich and coffee.'' He grinned. ''How does that sound to you?''

''Sounds okay,'' she said, matching his grin with her own. ''If you'll settle for grilled cheese and decaf coffee, I'll fix it for us at my apartment.''

''You're on,'' he said, grabbing hold of her hand. ''And now before we get caught in a shower of rain, let's get a taxi and head for your place.''

Tori unlocked her door and flipped the wall switch, illuminating her apartment in soft ivory light. Inwardly she heaved a relieved sigh to see that she'd left the living room in order, and the Sunday newspaper neatly folded on top of the coffee table.

''You've got a very nice place here, Tori,'' Max said, looking around, his admiring glance taking in the wicker chairs, glass topped brass coffee table and yellow slip-covered sofa that composed an attractive ensemble set off by the dark stained floor. The richly grained wood was polished to a glossy sheen and covered only in the area under the coffee table by an heirloom Persian rug. The basic color of the rug was rich royal blue covered with leaves, flowers and palmettes all geometrically stylized in shades of red, ivory and yellow. ''It's not only attractive, it suits you.''

The implied compliment in Max's voice pleased her. ''It's small, of course. But on the kind of rent I can afford I couldn't get both good location and size. This is the area I liked, and I stretched some to take it. That's why I furnished it on that proverbial shoestring they talk about,'' she said, hunching her shoulders in a theatrical manner.

Max looked amused. ''Don't you think you're overacting just a wee bit? Even an actress as good as you can't convince me she got this Persian rug on any shoestring.'' He pointed his index finger toward the floor.

She shrugged, but less dramatically this time. ''You're right. I didn't. I found that rug in a little antique shop in Brooklyn and something told me that if I didn't buy it I'd always be sorry. So I splurged to get one really lovely thing for my apartment and did the rest on that little old shoestring,'' she said, laughing.

There was a spiral wrought iron staircase leading from the living room to an upper level bedroom. Tori now led Max into a recessed area behind the stairs where there was a well laid out kitchen with a bay-windowed dining room.

''Would you like something to drink while I'm fixing supper, Max?''

''What have you got?''

''Only bottled water, I'm afraid. Look over there.'' She indicated a rack above one of the kitchen cabinets. ''I did a holiday television commercial last year for a natural spring water company and they sent me a case of their water.''

''No money—just paid you off in water, huh!''

''I got paid, silly. The water was a bonus.''

"Good. Glad to hear you were so well compensated for a talented performance before the TV cameras," Max said, restraining laughter.

"Now direct me to your glasses and we'll be in business."

"I'll get them and you can pour," she said, going over to a small buffet in the dining alcove and taking out a pair of amber colored stemmed glasses. "These are old Bohemian wine glasses and I found six of them at a flea market: two amber, two royal blue and two ruby red."

Max took the amber ones from her, with a grin of amusement. "Something else you bought on that shoe-string, no doubt."

"Better than that," she said, looking smug. "I swapped a piece of early American Sandwich glass in shell-and-tassel pattern for them."

"Since you sound so pleased about it, I take it that was a coup."

She tossed her head up, looking as satisfied as a cat that's been in the cream. "It was a beneficial trans-action for both of us. I got the glasses I wanted and the antique dealer got something she'll make a good profit on. We were both happy. And I might add that this is the very first time I've used them." She smiled with an air of pleasure.

"Then this is an occasion that calls for a special toast." He filled their glasses and handed one to Tori. Raising his to her, he said,

Let's toast today and embrace its shining hours.
For the secrets of our yesterdays are past,
and what tomorrow holds is yet unknown.
Only this day can we really call our own.

He clicked his glass lightly against Tori's as he finished the toast.

"Max, that's lovely. Is it from one of your plays?"

He shook his head. "I wish I could take the credit, but my father is the toast maker. It's one of his."

Tori couldn't conceal the interest quickening on her face. "Oh, then your father is a writer just like you?"

Max wagged his head negatively once again. "Dad is an English professor at the University of Vermont in Burlington. Although he doesn't write he's the one who guided me into playwriting. Actually pushed me, I should say." Max added with a snort and a chuckle. "The ol' professor had me writing skits and one acts from the day I entered high school. Then I went on to Columbia and completed two three-act plays by the time I graduated. Both of them were produced by the drama school there, and you can bet my dad took full credit. Claims to this day that my writing plays was all his idea. Why, that stubborn old Vermonter was a driving force behind me all the way from Burlington to Broadway, and he sure as heck enjoys telling you about it." There was a caring sound in his voice and he accompanied his words with a broad and warm smile.

"You're so fortunate to have someone approve so

much of what you do," Tori said wistfully. "How wonderfully proud your father is of you."

Max shot her a questioning look. "You saying your dad didn't want you to become an actress."

"I don't know what he might have wanted for me." She sighed, giving a little shiver because she had suddenly grown cold. "My father was killed in Vietnam a month before I was born. "I never knew a father's attention, nor felt a father's love." She hugged herself, clutching her arms and squeezing her tender flesh as an ache of longing spread through her. She had always wondered how it felt to be carried piggyback on a father's big masculine shoulders, or to walk through the park with her small hand tucked in his protective grip, or to stand outside the lion's cage at the zoo and not be frightened because he hugged her close to his side.

Unbidden tears filled her eyes thinking of all she'd been denied. She was never called princess, or daddy's little girl. Her father was never there even to call her by her name. She grew up hungering for warm hugs, reassuring pats and kisses. She had no father to give them, and her mother was so consumed with grief that she suppressed any displays of emotion.

Not wanting Max to see her tears, she had turned away and now she busied herself again with the supper. Max moved behind her and placed his hands on her shoulders.

"I'm sorry, Tori. Growing up never having known

your father was traumatic for you.'' His warm hands hugged her shoulders sympathetically. ''You did have a mother who encouraged you, I'm sure. She must be happy knowing your now playing on Broadway.''

''Perhaps she is, I don't know. She never tells me what she feels about me, or anything else actually.'' Her face became contemplative and still as she thought about her mother, and how best to explain the kind of person she was to Max. ''Mom is good and she's worked hard to provide me with all the material things I needed. I love her very much and she loves me too, of course. She's simply not someone who shows her emotions. The only thing I can say she wanted for me was to have me stand erect and walk well.'' Tori shrugged matter-of-factly. ''You see Mom has always been a high school gym teacher. Good posture was the big thing with her.'' Tori straightened her back in an automatic reflex, holding her head upright. ''You can't imagine how many hours I practiced walking with a book on my head.'' Her lips offered a small wintry smile. ''At least Mom was pleased about that. She does approve of the way I carry myself. I do know that much.''

Max leaned over and kissed the curve of her neck. ''I approve too. I liked the way you walked the first time I saw you. Remember?'' He feathered kisses along her neck and this light caress sent shivers of pleasure through her, causing her heart to thump for a second before settling back to its natural rhythm.

"Is that why you gave me the part in *Rowena's Daughter?*" She asked, easing away from his touch and turning to face him.

"That may have had something to do with it."

"Then if I practice walking with a book on my head for a few minutes every day can I maybe get a part in your next play?" There was a note of entreaty in her voice that she wasn't able to hide.

"I have to finish writing it before I can think about casting it," he said in a noncommittal tone of voice.

She looked away, momentarily rebuffed. Obviously she'd been unwise to approach Max about his plans for next season's play.

As if he realized that he'd sounded abrupt, Max quickly added, "I'm having problems with the final act of my new play. Too, I've always been superstitious about discussing my play before it's completed. So please understand and bear with a temperamental playwright. Can you do that?" he asked, his tight expression relaxing into an entreating smile.

"Why not," she managed to say offhandedly. She shrugged and turned her attention to slicing cheese for their sandwiches. Max's attitude puzzled her. It wasn't just his reluctance to talk about his plans for his next play. There was more to it than that. There was something he wasn't telling her. She got a disquieting feeling that she wouldn't be happy knowing what it was.

Chapter Four

The rest of March was windy and cool and the sun shed a watery light over the city. One could feel the approach of spring in the air, and in the faded cornflower sky, where a few clouds which seemed to come from the south floated lazily over the rooftops. When April came, the days were warmer and the little green swellings on the trees in Central Park broke into buds. Then soon the streets were touched with the softening magic of trees in leaf, and people strolled with no more aim than to look and smell the air.

Tori saw Max every night at the theater. Often he came by her dressing room and they talked while she put on her stage makeup. Many evenings following the performance they went out for coffee or a late supper. The only thing that they never did again was spend a Sunday together. Sunday was the day Max spent entirely with his daughter. Tori understood this, of course, but she thought after Robin had been back from Vermont for a couple of weeks that Max might include her in their Sunday brunch. That hadn't happened.

She had mentioned to him once that she'd like to meet and get to know Robin.

"When the play closes and we all have more time we'll see about that," he'd said.

She didn't question him, although she certainly couldn't figure his motive. He almost acted as if he were afraid to have her meet his daughter. Yet why on earth would that be? Such a thought was ridiculous. Tori dismissed it as quick as it came. After all, why should she make a problem out of Max wanting to wait until the play closed to have her get acquainted with Robin. Knowing Max it was like him to make a special scenario for this. Now having rationalized it to her complete satisfaction, Tori breathed a sigh of contentment and hurried through the wings to join Corinne on stage for the opening scene of tonight's play.

It is possible that Tori's performance that night was the best she'd ever given. Certainly there was a luminescent beauty in her face and eyes. This with the extraordinary mobility of her features had a magnetic impact on the audience.

After the final curtain call, Corinne threw her arms

around Tori, hugging her tightly. "You were superb! You had a special quality about you tonight." There was warmth in the praise of the older actress.

"Did I really?"

"You know you did. Just look at you. You're aglow." Corinne stepped back and viewed her fellow actress with a thoughtful smile. "You know, there's always one special night in the run of a play. One stellar performance. Often you can't define what made it so. It just is. I believe this was your special night for *Rowena's Daughter*. You were radiant, and you still are."

A warm flush colored Tori's face. "I do feel good about things. You're right, it's a special time for me in many ways." She felt the heat of the lights that still continued to bathe the stage in blue-white brightness. She fanned her face with quick waves of her hand.

Corinne seemed to study Tori with keen, discerning eyes. "It's more than the play, isn't it?"

Tori pressed her lips together and nodded.

An expression of troubled concern marked the older woman's face, dulling the amber luster of her expressive eyes. "Is it Max? Has he become that important to you?"

Tori's mouth softened, her lips parting in an enrapt smile. "More important than any man I've ever known before."

"Does Max know this?"

"No, I haven't told him how I feel," she answered,

no longer smiling. "I—I don't know how to say it—or even if I can. I've tried to hide my emotions. I think I'm afraid to let a person know how deeply I feel."

"But you do it on stage every night," Corinne said, frowning.

"I'm acting then. I can pour out all the emotions inside of me there because the audience wants it—accepts it—and accepts me." A pained expression pinched Tori's face. "You see, I never had that acceptance outside the theater. My mother never showed her feelings. She discouraged me from showing mine. She said I'd only end up being hurt." She crossed her arms across her breasts in a self-protective gesture. "I think this and the fact that I never knew my father has made it hard for me to have a significant relationship with any man I've known." She shook her head pensively. "Though I can't say it mattered very much until Max." She looked at Corinne, smiling softly. "Everything matters now with him."

There was the imperceptible sound of Corinne's quick intake of breath. "Oh my but you're vulnerable," she muttered tonelessly. "Yet in a lot of ways Max is vulnerable too." She gave a deep sigh which was instantly followed by fluttering movements of her hands as she played nervously with the rope of pearls around her neck. Throughout her acting career Corinne had always worn various strands of beads on stage as often as her part would allow it. And there had been times when she'd insisted on adding a necklace to her costume even when the director felt it was uncalled for. In her younger, more obvious days, Corinne had stolen scenes with a strand of pearls. She used them now as some people use cigarettes, nervously, an occupation for her trembling fingers.

"Max is special, but then so are you," the actress said finally, her voice rich as she picked up words again. "Well, that about sums it up, and I'd better hurry and get out of makeup. Griff will be waiting for me. He's a wonderfully patient man, but I hate to keep him waiting long." Her lovely forehead remained faintly creased as she turned and walked away from Tori into the wings.

Tori watched after her, feeling strangely moved. Her feeling for this celebrated actress was the sum of many things: admiration, friendship, genuine fondness, and gratitude for rare moments of almost maternal caring in Corinne's manner toward her.

This last thought made Tori pause, however, and admit the idea of motherly affection came from her own deep needs. She had never known this from her own mother, and she still suffered from its lack.

Yet, if Tori really thought about it, picturing Corinne as an actual mother of a child was incongruous. The acclaimed actress was just that: first, last and always an actress. Corinne typified the dedicated professional woman who put her career above all else. There would never have been a place in her life for a child. Tori wondered if this might explain why Corinne and Griff had never married.

Yet, even though Corinne did seem to live a self-centered sort of life, during these months since Tori joined the cast of *Rowena's Daughter* this magnificent star of the play had been constantly helpful and encouraging to her. She helped Tori to project her talents to a degree that earned her mention and praise from one of the New York drama critics. Corinne actually treated Tori as if she were her own special protégée. No wonder she felt boundless gratitude to the actress.

For all of these reasons it was important to her that Corinne should approve of her emotional involvement with Max. There had been moments here tonight when she sensed that Corinne had some reservations about it. Was it for her, or for Max, she wondered. Maybe it was her imagination, but there had been something troubling in Corinne's attitude when she'd told her how important Max had become to her. Tori couldn't quite put her finger on what it was. She had the feeling, however, that it was something concerning Max. After all, Corinne had starred in three of his plays. Too, she was godmother of his child. She was bound to know a great deal about him. What could she have meant in saying Max was vulnerable in many ways? She shuddered, feeling a dull ache of foreboding.

Well so she and Max were both vulnerable in some ways. That needn't spoil anything. She tossed her head up, dismissing the idea of Corinne's negative reaction, then hurriedly marched off stage.

In the hall Tori saw Griff Marland sitting on a dilapidated Romanesque bench outside of Corinne's dressing room. He sat with his legs stretched out, his fingers meeting at the tips and his forefingers touching his chin. "Hello, Tori," Griff acknowledged her with a smile. "Max spirited Corinne away from me the minute she came off stage. A curse on that younger, better looking man." His laugh was softly modulated, polite, what Tori had learned to expect from him, for he was a man sure of himself and a little amused with life.

"Younger, but no better looking." Corinne's crystal clear voice countered as she hurried toward him and slipped onto the bench beside him. "And like fruit-cake and brandy, everything improves with age, darling." She took his hand and all the lights came on behind her eyes. "Besides, I was only gone five minutes, and I left Max and came running back to you."

Tori walked on in the direction of her dressing room, knowing Corinne and Griff wouldn't even notice she had gone. She smiled thinking what a perfect man Griffith Marland was for Corinne. He loved her completely and devotedly, and never failed to be the audience for her at all times. He played the role she wanted him to play, the role that wasn't written in any book, that existed only in her mind. Griff had a surface softness, but there was strength in him, and character, despite the supporting role that he accepted in his relationship with Corinne. There was nothing jealous or mean in him. He had a tolerant attitude toward other people and it was a tolerance that didn't patronize. He was seldom astonished at anything that anyone did, but he was always interested. Griff liked people and admired talent, therefore he both liked and admired Max. Tori knew this. She also knew that Griff admired her performance in *Rowena's Daughter*. Maybe this was because Corinne praised her to him, but she wanted to think that, to a degree, it was that he saw talent in her acting.

At that moment all thought of Corinne and Griff vanished from her mind for she caught sight of Max standing in the open doorway to her dressing room waiting for her. He stepped toward her with his arms out and she rushed into them.

''You were glorious tonight,'' he said, hugging her warmly.

''Did you really think so?''

''Yes, I really did,'' he underlined each word emphatically. ''In fact, I'd say this was the best night in the entire run.''

She slanted her eyes up at him, fluttering her eyelashes coyly. ''Do you like me even better in the part than the first actress who played it?''

''I like you better period,'' he said, laughing and kissing her quickly before pushing her inside her dressing room. "Now get changed fast so we can go eat. I'm in the mood for a pecan waffle."

"Sweet and nutty. Sounds just like you." She wrinkled her nose, giving him an impish grin as she closed the door on him.

Toward the end of April Max announced to the cast that *Rowena's Daughter* would close at the end of the third week in May. Tori dreaded the thought of the play ending. She was afraid of the changes that might occur for her once she was no longer coming to the theater where Max was six nights out of seven. Unable to voice her fears to Max, because the relationship between them still remained undefined, she simply waited for him to tell her of his plans beyond the run of *Rowena's Daughter.* If he had plans for the summer he hadn't mentioned them to her. She imagined that he'd use all the summer months to finish writing his next play. And what of his new play? Would it, like his others, star Corinne? And would he consider her for a part in it too? She wished she could bring this up with him, but somehow she couldn't find an opportune time. Also, she remembered the one time when she'd asked about his play for next season and he'd cut her off. She had to be careful not to make that same mistake with him again.

Chapter Five

There is nothing ordinary about any performance by Corinne Hayes. Closing night of *Rowena's Daughter* was no exception. Corinne's acting skills performed magic. The nerves, the muscles, the delicate, invisible antennae of this widely experienced actress recalled each fine moment from every earlier performance of the play, and holding them like a mirror she reflected them as a fresh, new, sparkling image. When the play was over the curtain calls for the players were endless. The theater was like an Italian opera house on a gala night. The audience didn't want to let the cast go.

Max hovered at the edge of the stage beaming and exuding an air of pleasure and pride. The caterer had already arrived, and the champagne corks began to pop as soon as the cast assembled backstage for the closing night celebrations. Within a half hour the party's number swelled to include the actors' agents, several director and producer friends of Max and of course Griff and the other financial backers of the play.

Both Corinne and Tori were receiving praise for their performances. Accolades flew so fast and furiously no one could take them all in. Tori's agent, Jayson Klein, came up beside her offering her a glass of champagne.

"I trust you're not thinking about taking a vacation from work just because the run of this play has ended," he said.

She accepted the wine. "Why do you say that?" she asked, without looking directly at him. "Since I've worked hard these last four and a half months, don't you think I've earned a little rest and change of pace?"

"What you've earned is a special acting opportunity and a change of scenery." There was a knowing look in his eyes and a complacent smile on his broad face. "Want to hear about it?"

Tori looked at him quizzically, intrigued by his words and manner. "Of course I do, Jayson. You've got a look on your face like a Siamese cat and that makes me mighty curious. So what's up?"

"A rather meaty part in a television movie Tobias Parkman Productions is going to film on the West Coast," he said with a significant lifting of his brows.

Involuntarily Tori's fingers tightened around the

champagne glass she was holding. "What sort of movie is it?"

"I gathered from talking to the casting director yesterday that it's a blockbuster courtroom drama. The title is *The Third Witness*. They're looking for a talented young actress who's not one of the current Hollywood breed. You're a new face with plenty of talent. All I need is a go-ahead from you and I can have you signed up for this with one phone call to the coast." He gave her a conspiratorial grin. "What do you say?"

"I—I don't know." Tori's brow puckered in a frown. "It sounds good, and I'd really like to do a television movie. But I don't really want to go out to the coast." There was a pensive shimmer in the shadow of her eyes. "Right now I think I need to stay in New York."

"Why do you say that?" Surprise marked Jayson's words, giving them an angry sound. "There's nothing I can get for you right now in New York that has a fraction of the potential of this Parkman production. They're into a lot of the big miniseries, you know. You do a good job for them on this two-hour movie and they could consider you for something major later on. You've got to have enough savvy to see that, Tori." He leveled his finger at her. "Trust me. This is a fine opportunity for you."

She drew in her breath and let it out slowly. "You're right, I know. Only, there are some personal reasons why I don't feel I should be away from New York.'' She ran the tip of her tongue across her bottom lip. ''I just wouldn't be happy away from here right now.''

A dark frown pinched his heavy eyebrows drawing them together over the bridge of his prominent nose. Jayson was obviously put off by her attitude, and she couldn't blame him for that. She'd grabbed at every chance he'd tried to set up for her in the past. She could hardly expect him to accept the fact that all of a sudden she was placing something ahead of her career ambitions.

''I advise you to think about it over the weekend, you may just change your mind.'' He regarded her intently as he said this, challenging her with his keen blue eyes. ''My gut feeling is that you'll be sorry if you pass up a part in a television movie that Toby Parkman is producing.''

Tori could read the disappointment in Jayson's face. Her lack of interest irritated him. He was a good agent; he worked hard to open doors for her. He had a right to expect her cooperation, only this time he wasn't getting it. She knew she rated his anger.

''I'm sorry Jayson,'' she said contritely. ''I can't expect you to understand.'' She gave him a conciliatory smile before turning her head to search the room for Max. Right now she wanted to get away from Jayson, bring an end to their discussion before she alienated him further.

Tori spotted Max near the buffet table talking with Corinne, Griff and Monica Wells. As Tori joined them, Monica moved closer to Max leaving room for Tori to stand beside Corinne.

"Tori you're just in time to hear the plans Max has made for several of us to do eight weeks of repertory theater this summer at a charming little playhouse in the Catskills," Monica said, smiling first at Tori and then returning her full attention to Max. "I'm so excited to get to be one of the six players that will make up the company."

Tori gaped at Monica, then shot a surprised look at Max. "You never mentioned this," she said, a tremble in her voice revealing how stunned she was by Monica's statements. "I had no idea you were going to do any plays this summer, here or anywhere." She studied his inscrutable expression curiously. "When did all this come about?"

"It was actually my idea in the beginning," Griff spoke up before Max could give an answer. "I know that Corinne is happiest when she's busy acting. So I proposed the idea to Max way back in the winter. I got Max to agree to form a small company of actors if I located a playhouse and handled all the business details and accommodations for the group for July and August."

Ugly needles of suspicion were jabbing at Tori's mind. She fought to keep control of herself and not reveal the deep inner pain she was experiencing.

"Well it certainly seems that you and Griff accomplished exactly what you wanted," she said, looking at Max and forcing a smile across her trembling lips. "I'm sure it will prove an interesting and successful summer for everybody." She was watching him closely and she didn't miss the strained look in his eyes. He stood there saying nothing, everything about him was tense, his shoulders, the set of his mouth, his distressed, lined face. She straightened her shoulders and turned her attention to Corinne. "I just came over to say good-night to all of you. There're some folks waiting for me, so I must run." Turning abruptly on her heels, Tori held her head high and with as much dignity as she could summon walked away, all the time demanding that her eyes not well with tears.

Her mind churned with varied emotions as the shock and hurt of what she had learned filled her with humiliation and anger. Max had been planning this summer theater company for over four months without mentioning the slightest word about it to her, and he never would have. The reason was abundantly clear. Max's summer plans did not include her, in fact, it was most apparent to her now that none of Max's future plans would include her.

It was all becoming painfully real to her. She had deluded herself into thinking it was more, but the truth was that her little romance with Max had come about only because she was a fresh, new actress who for the past four months had seemed attractive to him simply because she was appearing in one of his plays. Max did not expect or want their relationship to develop into anything more than a romantic interlude during the run of the play. And this explained why he wouldn't discuss his play for next season with her. Next season was in the future; part of that unknown tomorrow that Max had spoken of in the toast he'd given that night in her apartment. She remembered how he lifted his glass to hers in a toast to the present. "Only this day is really ours," he'd said. Apparently he was stating his philosophy more clearly than she'd realized. When he'd told her to embrace today's shining hours it was because there were to be no tomorrows for her to share with him.

Tears stung the corners of her eyes and her hands flew to her face to hold back the sob erupting from her throat. For suddenly she fully understood why Max had never found a time to have her meet his daughter. He had no reason to want Robin to get acquainted with someone who was simply an actress in the play he was presently directing—someone who would never become an important part of his life.

Without needing to think about it, Tori instantly knew, without question, what she had to do. She'd always had an instinct for self-preservation. Fortunately it had never been stronger that it was at this moment.

She hurried forward, elbowing her way through the noisy party throng until she located her agent. "I do want you to get me that part in the Tobias Parkman movie,'' she declared in a clear, firm voice. ''I've just realized, Jayson, that I have the same gut feeling about this television opportunity that you do. I'd be a fool to hang on here in New York right now. So look out California, here I come!'' She laughed then, and there was a brittle sound in her laughter that was almost like hysteria.

Chapter Six

Two days later Tori boarded a plane for Los Angeles. The day after that the filming began on *The Third Witness.*

As Tori approached the studio early that morning, she felt a quickening inside, and her heart beat a little faster. Excitement tingled through her in short, sharp waves. Even the anguish she'd suffered over the past few days could not lessen or diminish these feelings. For she always felt this way when she went to work in a new role. The anticipation and the expectation mingled together at this moment and brought a smile of eagerness to her face.

Ever since she took up acting, the theater for her had been a place of refuge, and her happiest moments had been spent on stage. She knew it would be the same acting before cameras here in a studio lot. She would find escape from reality in her new role, and bring to it such belief and intensity that for the duration of the filming she would literally become the character she played.

Tori's role in *The Third Witness* was not a large one, yet she was the pivotal character in two highly dramatic courtroom scenes. The director took considerable time with her, pointing out important details of the technique of acting in front of a camera. These echoed ominously in her ears as she took her position for the first scene. She prayed, rather fervently, that she not be tempted to overact or be histronic, also that she not swing in the other direction and be too low-key to make the right impact. She must have hit just the right note and given a balanced performance, for the director looked well pleased. "Nice work," he said, giving her an approving nod. "That's a take."

The second of the major trial scenes was completed by the middle of the following week. At that time Tori was told that the only remaining scene for her would be shot outdoors on the steps of the courthouse followed by a brief view of her walking off down the street.

"We'll do that tomorrow and that will wind things up for you, Tori," the lean-faced director told her. "Oh, and by the way, your agent called this morning to find out when you might be through and could return to New York. Better call him tonight and let him know. He seemed eager for you to get back. My guess is he has something on the fire for you.''

Tori's eyes widened, registering her surprise. ''If he does, I haven't heard about it.'' Her smile was wistful. ''I sure hope he does though, because I'd like to be kept busy all summer. That would be the best thing that could happen to me.''

Eager to learn what was behind Jayson's inquiries about her, the first chance she got she called his office. It was late in the afternoon and she knew that meant it was well after five o'clock in New York, but she hoped she'd be lucky and find him still working. The phone rang four times without an answer. She let it keep ringing and a few seconds later he answered.

''Jayson, it's Tori. Gee, I was getting afraid I wasn't going to catch you.''

''You almost didn't. I had left, but then I discovered it was just starting to rain. I came back to pick up my umbrella and heard the phone.'' He paused, just long enough to catch his breath. ''What's up, Tori?''

''That's what I called to ask you. Heard you were asking when I'd be through filming and back in New York.''

''Yeah. I checked today as a matter of fact, and they couldn't tell me where you were staying. I went through a glib-talking but know-nothing receptionist, some flunky on the set of your movie, and finally was allowed a one-minute conversation with your director. I didn't find out anything that I really needed to know.

Needless to say, I'm more than thankful that you called.'' He punctuated his words with an audible sigh of relief.

''You're certainly building my curiosity to a new high. So tell me, what is it you wanted, anyway?''

''Well, let me sit down and I'll tell you.'' He cleared his throat and didn't say anything for a moment. Tori could picture Jayson carrying the telephone while he circled his desk and sank down in his favorite leather chair. ''Max Branton has been after me trying to find out where on earth you were. Seems you didn't bother to tell him you were going out to the coast to work on the Parkman movie. Why didn't you?''

''I didn't see any reason to,'' she said tersely. ''And he didn't ask me about my plans for the summer.''

''Well he's asking now.''

''He is. Why?''

''He's eager to have you take Monica Wells' place in his summer theater group. That's why.''

Tori gripped the phone. ''Wh—what happened with Monica?'' She asked with a quick intake of breath.

''I don't know all the details. She had some sort of accident. Caught her foot in a grate over a storm sewer, I think he said. Anyway she ended up fracturing some bones in her foot and breaking her ankle.''

''Wow! Sounds bad.''

''Bad enough to keep her away from the Playhouse in Summerville,'' he exclaimed, a verbal shrug in his tone. "So now Max's is counting on you to take her place."

Tori didn't say anything for a long moment. When she did her uneven voice mirrored the uncertainty she felt. "I—I don't know, Jayson. I'm not too sure I'd fit in with the others in his group."

"Of course you would. Why you know darn well Corinne Hayes would have picked you over Monica in the first place."

"Could be, but what about the others. Do you know who they are?"

"I know about two of the men. One is even a client of mine. He's a fine young actor named Lon Taylor. He was relatively unknown until last season. Then he won critical acclaim in the revival of that Eugene O'Neill play. They said he combined the talent of a young Marlon Brando with the sensitivity of the legendary James Dean." Jayson's voice crescendoed as he related his clients talents. "You'll like Lon. I guarantee it."

"He sounds great. I only wish I'd seen the O'Neill revival," she said, echoing his enthusiasm. "Now who's the other actor you know about?"

"Brandon Fiske, the movie actor," he said wryly.

"Heavens, he's quite a celebrity. Not bad looking either," she added laughing. "All the women will flock in to see him."

"Yeah, he's a crowd pleaser. I bet that's why Max hired him. 'Cause he's no great shakes as an actor. He can only play one part and that's Brandon Fiske,'' he scoffed. ''At any rate it'll be an interesting two months of theater for you. You'll be working with Max and a good group of fellow actors. I thought you'd jump at the chance. That is if you get through out there in time, and from what your director said this morning I got the idea you'll be finished in another day or two.''

''That's right. I have only one more scene and it's scheduled for tomorrow.''

''Good! Timing should work out about right. Max said the first play will open on the third of July and he wants everyone at Summerville five days ahead to rehearse. So what do you say? Shall I negotiate your contract?''

She hesitated for a long moment trying to suppress the storm of mixed emotions that had been racing through her mind. This is an eight-week acting job, she told herself. And acting was what she did. If she was a true professional now was the time for her to prove it. She cleared her throat. ''Yes,'' she said, and her voice didn't waver a bit. ''You can tell Max I'll be happy to be a part of his summer theater company. Tell him I'll be in Summerville right on schedule.''

As Tori hung up the telephone she made a silent vow to bury her personal feelings, and from this moment on to make certain that everything between her and Max be on a strictly business basis. He was the director of the plays in which she would perform and nothing more. She could not, and must not, forget that fact for a single minute. For if she did, Max Branton would surely break her heart.

Chapter Seven

Summerville was not a town. Nor could it even be labeled a village. It was a resort hamlet nestled between rock- and tree-covered mountains and overlooking a deep blue lake. Tori parked the Ford Escort she'd rented near the front of the three-story alpine lodge and climbed out into the shimmering sunlit afternoon. She glanced around, her eyes eagerly absorbing the surroundings. The rustic wood and stone hotel was situated at the head of the lake with the imposing emerald green mountains behind it. The Catskills are beautiful in every season, especially so in June and July when the laurel blooms. Like confetti, the pink and white blossoms were scattered everywhere.

In addition to the main lodge, there were half a

dozen guest cottages secluded among the many trees in an area that sloped down to the edge of the lake. The seclusion of one of the cottages held no appeal for Tori, so she had opted for staying in the chalet-styled lodge.

As soon as she had checked in, she was shown to the oversized room on the third floor that Griff had reserved for her. She uttered an exclamation of satisfied delight at its old world charm and new world spaciousness. The room had a vaulted ceiling ribbed with heavy walnut stained beams. While the walls were white, the carpet and draperies were Dutch blue. Mock canopies formed a headboard for the alcoved bed. Blue and white toile print fabric was stretched between two of the dark wood beams attaching the canopy to slender tension rods at the top. The same material was used for the bedspread, and the effect was that of a scene on a Delft tile from Holland.

A sitting room area was created at one side of the room with a pair of blue lounge chairs and a large square lamp table. There was also a small deck off the bedroom from which Tori had a panoramic view of all of Summerville. It was totally to her liking, and as the porter deposited her two suitcases on luggage stands, she thanked him and gave him a generous tip.

Without any delay she opened her luggage, taking out a comfortable pair of walking shoes. There would be ample time to unpack her clothes tonight. Right now she was interested in exploring her surroundings and checking out the playhouse. She had already determined that the theater had to be the low building a couple of hundred yards to the left of the lodge.

About ten minutes later, Tori was trying the double doors at the front of the theater. Finding them securely locked, she walked around the building, hoping the windows along the side would be set low enough to the ground that she could look through and get a glimpse of the interior. She discovered, however, that the narrow, oblong panes of glass were set high in the redwood wall. Continuing around to the rear, she came on what must be the stage door. It stood slightly ajar. A frail glow of light issued from a glass-shaded light bulb in the ceiling of the backstage area. She entered and walked rapidly down the dimly lighted passage that brought her through the wings and onto the stage.

Several flats had been put up, and the set appeared to be partially assembled. She should have expected that. Max would have ordered the set and props to be ready for the first read through of the play. With his penchant for having things exactly on time, he'd have made darn sure the scenery arrived ahead of the players. She gave an amused chuckle.

With her usual purposeful steps Tori crossed from one side of the slightly dusty stage to the other.

Then she walked to the back of the set, turned slowly and moved forward to center stage front. All her movements were calculated to give her a feel for the dimensions of this new stage she would be working on.

"You sure do have that harmony of movement when you walk, Tori."

She spun around, staring into the wings from where Max's voice had come. "You—you startled me," she stammered, crossing her arms across her chest as if she needed to shield herself from him. "How long have you been standing there?"

"Not long."

"You should have let me know you were in here."

"Why?" He walked toward her, an amused expression on his face. "I've told you before that you had nice moves. I was enjoying watching you."

She assumed a belligerent stance. "I didn't know anyone was in this theater but me. It's annoying to discover you've been looking at each step I took. I don't like being watched."

Max laughed at her. "That's ridiculous. You're an actress. Either you're watched or you're dead."

He stood facing her now so she stepped away, moving to the front edge of the stage and peering out at the rows of seats. "And just how many would the clever director say will watch me from this stage in the next few weeks?"

"Count the seats for yourself. We'll play to a full

house most every night.'' If there was sarcasm in his words, he masked it with a matter-of-fact tone.

Tori felt suddenly contrite. She was the one who had started sparring with him, and without cause or reason. She gritted her teeth, determined to quit over-reacting to every word Max said. ''Full house sounds good to me. Summerville must be a popular place here in the Catskills.'' She turned back as she said this, facing him again, a faint smile making her appear less tense.

''Always has been, I understand. And with the quality actors in our group we'll draw in the crowds. I can guarantee you that.'' He boasted, thrusting his hands in his trouser pockets. ''And speaking of our talented performers, I want to say that you're a very welcome addition. I'm glad you agreed to join us,'' he said, his mouth twisting up in his nice crinkly smile.

''And I'm glad you thought of me when Monica had to drop out,'' she replied evenly. ''Having an acting job for this summer is what I needed. When one thing comes to an end there's a letdown feeling. It can help if you start something else right away. At least it works that way for me.'' She met Max's direct gaze and attempted to smile. ''I'll get out of your way now so you can do whatever you need to do in here. I want to walk down to the lake and look around a bit.''

''You do that,'' Max said, shrugging. He continued to look at her, his hands plunged deep in his pockets.

Strangely, Tori had the feeling that he did this to keep from putting a restraining hand on her arm. But of course that was ridiculous, because if he had wanted her to stay in the theater with him, he would have asked her.

After she left Max at the playhouse, Tori followed one of the asphalt paths that meandered through the trees to the lake front. She took her time, pausing now and again to admire clusters of purple-red trilliums and breathe in the fragrance of waxy white pipissewa blossoms.

The path ended where a wooden dock extended some fifteen feet out onto the lake. A couple of small fishing boats were tied up to one side. There was no one around the dock, but a short distance out on the lake a lone fisherman was fishing from a row boat with an outboard. He sat there quietly, the motor stilled, the boat undulating gently with the movement of the water. Tori sat down at the end of the dock to watch him. Every now and then she could see him reel in his line and toss it out again on the opposite side of the boat. She had only been watching him a short time when suddenly his line jerked and his rod curved in a deep arc, the tip dipping into the water. With a deft motion the fisherman set the hook, then reeled in what appeared to be a sizeable bass. Since the boat was a short distance away, Tori reasoned that unless the fish was of fair size she wouldn't be able to see it at all. Definitely she'd label this one a keeper, she thought, smiling to herself, and hoping that while she was here at Summerville she could borrow a rod and reel and try her luck.

The grinding sound of the fisherman starting up his outboard shattered the still air. Not wanting to be sitting on the dock if the man were heading back to shore, Tori stood up, walked briskly off the dock, and began to climb back up the hillside path the way she'd come. It seemed a steeper incline going up than it had going down. She climbed slowly, pausing a second or two to keep from getting winded.

She passed within a few yards of one of the guest cottages just as a man came out and closed the door behind him. She didn't turn her head to look at him. Instead she quickened her steps trying to get beyond the point where the gravel walk from his cottage intersected the wider main path.

His long legs and lengthy stride gave him the advantage. He managed to intercept and force her to stop or collide with him.

"Tori Trent, I presume," he said, stepping directly in front of her, forcing her to look directly up into his dark, inquiring eyes. "Forgive me for stopping you so abruptly, but Max told me you'd arrived and I was on my way to find you and offer to buy you a drink. You and I are the first of our group to get here. I'm—"

"Brandon Fiske," she interrupted him. "And I don't presume that, I know it," she said, smiling. "I recognize you from your films.'' She stepped sideways indicating she wanted to get around him and go on up the hill. ''You said Max told you I was here. When did you come?'' She asked as Brandon aligned himself with her so they could walk side by side.

''About an hour ago. Max indicated that Corinne Hayes and Jill and Gordon Gentry were due in before six, but I don't know about Lon Taylor. I've never seen him. Do you know him?''

She shook her head. ''No, I don't know anyone other than Corinne.''

''You know me,'' he quipped.

''I know *about* you. Brandon Fiske, movie star, idolized by scads of female fans—if what the magazines print is true. That's not to know you as a fellow actor, which is the way I know Corinne.'' She was intentionally candid with him.

''We start being fellow actors tomorrow at our first rehearsal, so I think we should start to know each other tonight over dinner.'' He cupped his hand under her elbow to assist her as the path took a sharper incline.

Tori sidled an amused glance at his handsome profile. ''Five minutes ago you said you were looking for me to buy me a drink. How did you get beyond that to dinner so fast?''

Brandon looked at his watch. ''It took me six and a half minutes,'' he said, his black eyes sparkling with silent laughter. "You will agree to both a drink and dinner won't you?"

Brandon had a captivating manner, Tori wouldn't deny that. "I'll agree with pleasure," she said, as they reached the steps leading to the entrance to the lodge. "But you'll have to give me twenty minutes. I've been tramping around the lake and I want to change my shoes and freshen up a bit."

"You look fine to me just the way you are." His eyes swept over her in approval. "However, I won't argue with my new found fellow actor over just twenty minutes. Actually I'll use that time to check on a couple of things Max wanted me to see about while he's away."

Tori looked puzzled. "Max is here. Why I saw him at the theater."

"Yeah, I saw him there too. That's when he told me you'd arrived."

"Then isn't he still here now?"

Brandon shook his head. "He took off right after I saw him. Said he might not get back until late tonight.

A curious frown narrowed Tori's eyes. "How strange. I wonder where he went."

"He mentioned something about a girl's camp that was about fifty miles from here. Said his daughter was coming in on the camp's chartered bus and he wanted to be there to meet her." Brandon pulled the lodge door open for her as he related this. "I was a bit surprised. I don't think I'd heard him mention having a family before. Did you know he had children?''

''I knew he had a daughter, but I've never seen her. I understand his wife died a few years ago.'' She stated this quietly without a trace of emotional inflection in her voice. Then before Brandon might carry the subject of Max's family further, Tori hurried away to get ready for dinner.

Chapter Eight

" "W hen Max told me you'd be in our theater company this summer I cheered. Didn't I, Max?" It was a rhetorical question and Corinne flashed him a smile and went on talking. The three of them were the only ones in the playhouse as yet, for it was still fifteen minutes before the time Max had scheduled the first play rehearsal. "I actually shouted 'hallelujah,' " Corinne continued, extending her arms in a dramatic gesture, reminiscent of an enthusiastic evangelist at a revival meeting. "That was exactly my reaction at hearing the good news, wasn't it Max?" Corinne sustained her theatrical pose as she directed herself to Max.

"With a few embellishments that we've learned to expect from you, dear lady." He taunted her with an arch look.

Corinne gave a self-depricating laugh. "I was just glad that you had the good sense to include Tori. The point is that she needs to know that she's the perfect choice. She deserves to hear it from you Max. So tell her—right here and right now." Corinne's voice was low-pitched yet firm, even commanding.

Max glowered at her, anger coloring his face. "Egads, Corinne. Drop the ridiculous queen mother role. It's sure out of character for you."

Tori gasped, her eyes flaring in surprise. It was the first time she'd ever heard Max speak a harsh word to Corinne. Why his volatile reaction? Tori's troubled expression intensified as she looked from Max to Corinne. The actress had begun to twist her fingers through the long gold chain she wore looped around her neck, and a look of pain contorted her expressive face.

At that moment Brandon and the Gentry couple entered the playhouse. A second later Lon Taylor hurried in after them. Max did not speak directly to any of them. Rather, with that characteristic gesture of his, he pushed back his shirt cuff and looked at his watch.

"Everyone's on time," he announced in a sharp, authoritative voice. "Take your places on stage for act one and let's go to work."

For the first rehearsals of *Another April* Max stressed characterization, and concentrated on the pacing of the more dramatic scenes in relation to the lighter ones. A final dress rehearsal was scheduled for

Thursday night, as the play would open on Friday. On Thursday afternoon Max asked Brandon and Tori to play through their love scene in detail, since previously they had done the scene omitting the embrace and kiss called for at the end of the play.

"Let's take it from just after Tori has said good-bye to Corinne," Max ordered. "Don't enter the room though, Brandon, until Tori has had plenty of time to cross over to the piano and lower the cover over the keyboard. Prolonging this moment for Tori will add significance to your final scene."

Max had been standing at the edge of the stage. He now took a seat out front, watching intently as the two people on stage began the scene. His expression inscrutable as he concentrated his attention on the emotion-packed scene unfolding before him. Other than to take his chin between his thumb and forefinger, he didn't move a muscle until it was finished. Then he stood up, shaking his head slowly.

"Brandon you upstaged Tori from the middle of this scene through to the end. That's wrong. The power and the passion, you lose it all. You just throw it away." He leaped onto the stage and stood confronting the two of them. "It's important that before the kiss the audience has to be able to see Tori's face. Read the forgiveness in her expression." Max elbowed Brandon to one side and stepped in close to Tori. "Above all, it's vital that everyone out there in the audience can get a clear view, behold the gesture of loving acceptance in the way Tori lifts her face to receive your kiss."

Max took hold of Tori, positioning her so that she faced toward the audience. "Like this," he said, taking her in his arms and drawing her close, but making certain that her face still remained in clear view.

Tori looked at Max, her eyes wide and unblinking. What was happening here? "Look at me, Tori," Max whispered. "Look at me with forgiveness in your eyes. Then slide your arms around my neck." He paused, waiting for her to comply, his brilliant eyes locked with hers. "Now, lift your face to mine to show you accept the love I'm offering you."

Tori moved as if hypnotized by his eyes and his words. Max's arms tightened around her. His lips met hers, and he kissed her ardently and without restraint. The tumult of emotion that assaulted Tori's senses swept away any control she might have had. She clung to him, meeting his passion head on, oblivious to all else except the sensations his touch sent surging through every part of her.

There was a hushed silence on the stage which neither of them was aware of. Max took his lips from hers finally, moving his head away so he could look at her. Their eyes met and locked, and they both saw the longing and desire clearly revealed in the other's face.

Tori felt momentarily staggered. Then her lips parted slightly. She wanted to say his name, but it choked in her throat. She could only continue to stare at him speechlessly, letting her adoration of him blaze in her face. His eyes bored into her, devouring her and she returned his gaze unwaveringly until Brandon suddenly applauded and the rest of the cast joined him.

"That was effective Max. You really made your point. You certainly showed the way to get the most emotional power out of that final scene," he said, stepping forward and taking hold of Tori's hand, pulling her away from Max. "Okay, Tori, what do you say you and I try it once more with feeling." He grinned circling her waist with his arm and hugging her to him.

"Save it for tonight's dress rehearsal Brandon," Max said tersely. "We're through here for the afternoon." Max turned sharply on his heels and headed rapidly off the stage.

Tori's eyes were averted and she was determined to keep them so. She would not look after Max to see if he continued down the aisle and out of the playhouse. Rather with deliberate movements she disengaged herself from Brandon, and proceeded to walk around the stage set picking up a piece of sheet music that had fallen on the floor. Once she had set it back on the music rack, she lifted the cover that she had closed over the piano keys earlier when she was rehearsing the scene with Brandon. She tried not to think about what had happened between her and Max. Instead she squared the piano bench, leveled the picture which hung above the mantle, and carried two glasses and a decanter off the set to the prop table in the wings, acting like a fluttery parlor maid in a Victorian melodrama.

''That's enough Tori,'' Corinne said, laying a restraining hand on Tori's arm. ''Everyone's left.''

''Max too?''

Corinne nodded. ''He left immediately. Once he'd discarded the tight rein he'd kept on himself with you, what else could he do?''

''Nothing I suppose. I don't know why I asked.'' She sighed, shaking her head.

''You asked because you want to understand Max.''

''Well, I know better than to think I will, because I actually know very little about him. He's the most private man I think I've ever known.''

''Exactly, and that's why he called a halt on this rehearsal today. He's always hidden his personal life and emotions from the people he works with. Today he didn't. So before Brandon and the others might speculate on that highly charged scene you two were playing up there, Max rang the curtain down.''

Tori felt heat flaming her face. ''How transparent was I?'' she asked, running her hand inside the collar of her blouse and massaging the corded muscles at the back of her neck.

''If you want to know what the cast saw, it was a skilled actress being led by her director through a love scene so emotionally powerful that illusion seemed reality. Which is, after all, what happens in great moments in the theater.'' Corinne regarded her gravely, her forehead faintly creased. ''I saw something else, something more. Do you want me to tell you what that was?''

The steady regard of Corinne's thoughtful eyes made Tori uncomfortable, but she didn't look away. ''Yes, of course I do,'' she answered, her own eyes anxious, questioning.

''One night during *Rowena's Daughter* I asked you if Max Branton had become important to you. You told me then that he was more important than any other man you'd ever known. And he still is. Your feelings about him are even stronger than they were then. That's what I saw this afternoon, Tori.''

Tori's face was opalescent; the shadows under her eyes were like tear stains. ''That's enough. Don't say any more. I wish I hadn't asked you to tell me what you saw, or thought you saw,'' she said in a low, tormented voice. She made a move to indicate she was going to leave. She hesitated though, because she knew Corinne had spoken out of concern for her. ''My feelings are my problem. I'll find the best way to deal with them.'' She managed to push what she hoped was a convincing smile across her lips. ''As for anything else, Max is important to my acting career. He was while I played in *Rowena's Daughter*; he is now in this summer theater. It ends there.''

Corinne's tea-colored eyes were grave. ''That will change.''

"I seriously doubt that. Max doesn't want it to change. If he did he would have asked me in the beginning to work here with him this summer. But he asked Monica, and the plain and simple truth is Max didn't care enough about furthering a relationship between us to want me here."

"I disagree," Corinne said. "Did it ever occur to you that it's not because Max doesn't care enough. It's because he cares too much."

"That doesn't make sense," Tori said, frowning.

"It makes sense to Max." There was a melancholy note in Corinne's voice and there was sadness in her eyes.

Tori felt confused, not only by Corinne's statements, but by her emotional reactions whenever she talked about anything that concerned Max. "I'm afraid nothing makes sense to me right now. I don't understand Max's actions, and I certainly don't know what he's feeling. But if he wants me to know, he's going to have to be the one to tell me." With this, Tori turned to leave the stage. "Come on, Corinne. I'll walk back to the lodge with you," she added, her voice subdued and without inflection as she attempted to hide the distress she was feeling.

Another April opened the following night before a well-filled house. Griff had driven up from New York to see the performance. Tori's agent called to say he couldn't make it till later, but when he did come he was bringing a New York producer who had expressed an interest in both Tori and Lon Taylor. At lunch that day, Tori asked Lon if Jayson had mentioned anything about this to him.

"It's about a new Neil Simon play for next season," Lon told her. "Jayson said they're keeping it under wraps until Simon makes his own suggestions. Seems he likes to have a say in casting his plays." He offered this information in a confidential tone as if he were sharing an important secret with her.

"That's very interesting," she whispered back. "So we'll keep this just between the two of us."

He grinned, a boyish, disarming crinkling of his lean face. "Strictly the two of us," he said with a conspiratorial wink. Though he was not handsome in the given sense of that word, still a number of unusual qualitites combined to lift Lon Taylor out of the ordinary. He was a pleasant looking fellow with a fair complexion, light brown hair that was soft and straight, and a lean eager face. He had a generous mouth and his dove blue eyes were for the most part illuminated with humor and good will. "You know Tori, the two of us together in a play for next season, I'd be one hundred percent for that."

"Eighty-five percent, Lon. Don't forget, Jayson gets his fifteen percent off the top," she bantered, laughing.

The mood of the cast was exuberant Saturday night. The curtain came down on the kind of applause that every actor is sustained and nourished by. Thunderous.

It descended, rose again, and the performers returned to the stage one by one—the bit players, Jill and Gordon, the second male lead, Lon, then Tori, Brandon and Corinne. The clapping spiraled upward and the entire cast linked hands and bowed again.

Backstage after this, Brandon announced in his sonorous actor's voice, "This calls for a celebration; the party is on me. Everybody come to my cottage as soon as you're out of costume."

Tori heard Corinne beg off. She felt inclined to do the same, but she had no reason not to go. She could even risk offending the others if she excluded herself. She shrugged. Where was her *esprit di corps?*

Max must have sensed her reluctance. "Brandon's expansive mood won't allow no for an answer, Tori. So I'll wait for you to change. We can go down to his cottage together."

She nodded her agreement as she headed for the dressing room.

Knowing how Max disliked waiting, she creamed off her heavy stage makeup all the time picturing him impatiently stealing glances at his watch. When all traces of grease were wiped from her face, she splashed her skin with cool water before putting on a touch of eye makeup and a coral lipstick.

She'd worn yellow slacks with a matching cotton knit top to the playhouse tonight, so unless she returned to the lodge she would have to wear it on to the party. She liked yellow, wore it often in fact, but she knew green was her most becoming color. If she'd known ahead that she'd be with Max after the performance tonight, she have worn the mint green sun dress she'd bought while she was out in Hollywood. Making a face at herself in the mirror, she stood up. Her thoughts were absurd and so was she. Thrusting her feet into a pair of white canvas espadrilles, she rushed out to join Max at the front door of the playhouse.

"I didn't take too long now did I?" She approached him, drawing a white sweater over her shoulders as she stepped outside.

"Not too long," he answered, an admiring look in his eyes. "You're worth waiting for anytime, anywhere." His smile was warm and the caring look in his eyes at that moment seemed to take her breath away.

Max took her arm and they began walking down to Brandon's cottage. A light wind shook the trees and the sound caused Tori to look up. There were stars in the sliver of sky between the tree tops, and they seemed to give off a bluish light. On both sides of the path the tall evergreens stretched skyward, their feathery branches brushing the tender blue-tinged darkness.

Just as they reached Brandon's cottage, Max tightened his hold on her hand and held her back several steps from the door. "Don't go in until I tell you about tomorrow," he said, as he put both hands on her shoulders to keep her from moving away from him.

"Tomorrow is Sunday. No performance and no rehearsal, or have you forgotten your own schedule?" she asked with a questioning frown.

"I know it's Sunday. I'm not talking about work. I'm talking about a favor I'd like you to do for me."

Tori eyed him warily. "Why do I get the feeling you're about to put something over on me?"

"Not at all," he said, his expression totally serious. "I simply want you to help me keep a promise I made to Robin."

Her mouth dropped open in surprise. For the mention of his daughter was the last thing she could have expected right then. "What sort of promise?"

"I promised I'd visit her at camp tomorrow and bring a wonderful actress with me." The beginning of a smile tipped the corners of his mouth. "You see, she told her fellow campers that I'm a director of plays on Broadway and that I was going to bring a real actress for all of them to meet." He smoothed her shoulders as he explained.

Tori was finding the warmth of his caressing hands disconcerting. "Corinne is the celebrity. Take her."

"You're the one who's going to be in a television movie. You're the actress these young girls will get a thrill out of meeting."

"That gives a boost to my ego, but I think you're overstating it a bit. Besides, I imagine Robin expects Corinne to come with you."

His dark earnest eyes sought hers. "I've wanted you

and Robin to meet for some time now. I've already told her about you and she'd counting on your being there tomorrow. Please say you will.'' His voice was full of entreaty. ''Don't disappoint both Robin and me.''

Was this true? Had he told Robin about her? If he had, then truly he did want them to know each other. Her mouth curved into an unconscious smile. ''In that case, of course I'll go,'' she said softly. ''I really want to.''

There was a spark of some indefinable emotion in his eyes. ''I'm glad,'' he said. Then he stepped closer to the door and knocked to announce their arrival.

Chapter Nine

Sleepy Hollow Camp for girls was an hour's scenic drive from Summerville. Tori felt the massive presence of the surrounding hills as they followed the climbing road. The sky was saphire blue overhead, traversed by ballooning white clouds traveling at a leisurely pace.

Max told her when they were less than ten miles from the camp. At that point the road wound steadily downhill between steep pine covered mountainsides. A small river kept them company, chuckling and sparkling on its way in a series of little pools and waterfalls. At the end they turned a final corner and ahead lay a glittering, silvery lake and all the rustic log buildings of the Sleepy Hollow campsite.

Robin apparently had been waiting for them on the

porch of the mess hall. For as soon as Max stopped the car and slid out of the drivers seat, she came flying to greet him. She was a slender reed of a girl with a scrubbed immaculate look and an outdoors sort of face. Her hair was silky, straight and long, red-brown in color like the mane of a chestnut bay colt. She smiled joyously now at the sight of her father, her sweet, expressive mouth displaying a dimple at one corner.

"You're the first, the very first parent to come," she piped, her voice shrill with excitement, her freckle-spattered nose wrinkling disarmingly. "I'd have died if you'd been late. I hate so to wait."

Tori suppressed a smile at this. Robin was just like Max in that respect, she thought. Max beckoned Tori closer so he could introduce her to his daughter.

"Robin this is Tori Trent, the actress I told you about who's at the Summerville Playhouse with me."

The young girl's eyes, which were a shade lighter blue than her father's, widened as she looked intently into Tori's face. "You're on television too, aren't you?"

Tori nodded. "I'm going to be soon. I have a small part in a movie for television. They just finished shooting it so it will be a while I guess before it's shown."

"I've never met a television star before. This is so neat."

"I'm not a star, Robin. This is my first TV role," Tori said modestly.

"That's okay. Aunt Corinne is a big star and she's never been on TV at all," Robin stated with youthful candor.

This surprising mention of Corinne in this connotation floored Tori. "Corinne is the finest actress I know, but I certainly didn't know she was your aunt."

"She's really my great aunt, but she says that makes her sound ancient. So I can't say that. I usually tell people she's my aunt and favorite actress."

"Corinne is everybody's favorite," Max interjected before Tori might question Robin further about her kinship with the celebrated actress. He immediately put one arm around his daughter's shoulder, grabbing Tori's arm with his other hand. "Come on you two. Let's go have a look around this camp. I want to see and hear about all the things you've been doing, and I'm sure you'd like to introduce your cabin mates to Tori."

Robin required no prodding to take charge. She appeared totally delighted to have attention focused on her camp activities. The following hour or so was taken up with viewing all the various camp facilities. As Max had predicted, when the other young campers saw Tori, they were agog at having a Broadway actress in their midst.

A clamoring and eager group crowded around Tori asking questions and seeking autographs. Robin stayed close at her side assuming a proprietary attitude. Meanwhile, Max went to have a talk with the camp director to see if they could arrange a time when the campers could be brought over to Summerville to see a performance of the upcoming play.

There were a few minutes of high merriment when identical twins confused Tori, making her think that she was being asked to sign a second autograph for the same girl. It seems it was a constant sport at the camp for the twins to play tricks on an unsuspecting guest or counselor. All the girls were still laughing about this when one chubby camper wearing cut-off jeans and an extra large Camp Sleepy Hollow sweatshirt pushed her way into the circle around Robin and Tori.

"You played a trick on us, too, Robin. You said your mother was an actress on the stage, but you didn't tell us she was in television. Why didn't you?" she demanded in her strident voice.

Robin looked flustered, her face reddening. "Be—because Tori's not my mother," she stammered. "But my mother was an actress. She went to lots of different places—and she danced and sang in a whole gob of plays. But—she's dead now," she said bluntly, tears springing up in her eyes.

The round-faced girl looked embarrassed. "Geez! I'm sorry. I thought since she came with your father—this being parent's day and everything."

Tori spoke up quickly. "I'm one of the actresses in a theater company that Robin's father directs. Luckily the playhouse is close enough to camp, so I could come along with Mr. Branton to see Robin and meet all of her friends,'' Tori explained, bestowing a benign smile on this callow kid. Tori stood up then, extending her hand to Robin. ''We'd best go find your dad now. He's going to wonder what happened to us.'' Taking Robin's small hand, she gripped it warmly and immediately led her away.

Robin walked with her head down and didn't say anything until they were well out of earshot of the young campers. ''Did you ever know my mother?'' she asked shyly, lifting her head and shaking her hair back from the sides of her face.

''No, Robin. I'm afraid I didn't. Actually, I only met your father a few months ago when I tried out for a part in his last play.''

''Yeah, I know that. Daddy told me you were in the play with Aunt Corinne.''

''That's right.'' Tori felt a warm glow flow through her to learn that Max had spoken of her to his daughter.

''He said you were real good in the play, and that Aunt Corinne thought so too.''

Tori felt her face flush with pleasure. ''That's great to hear. Thank you for telling me. You know, I feel very lucky to have acted in one of your father's plays.''

''My mother was never in any of Daddy's plays.''

''She wasn't?'' There was a surprised inflection in Tori's voice.

"No. she didn't want to be," Robin responded matter-of-factly. "Aunt Corinne said it was because Mother liked to sing and dance all the time, and, of course, Daddy's plays weren't that kind."

"It sounds like your mother was an actress in what we call musical theater. Plays like *Phantom of the Opera, Cats,* and *A Chorus Line.*"

"I guess so. I don't know the names." She frowned. "She was away a lot. Now it's hard to remember much about the times she was home." Saying this her glowing youthful face paled and a look of sadness passed over her small features. She glanced up at Tori. "You don't go to a lot of cities to act in plays do you?"

"No, I've never been in a road company. I've only done plays in New York and now this summer up here in the Catskills."

"Well, don't ever start doing that 'cause my daddy wouldn't like it if you did," she said, looking at Tori, her expressive eyes solemn like a little owl's.

Tori was dumbfounded by Robin's statement. Before she could come up with any sort of reply, Max appeared, right on cue, as if this were a pivotal scene in one of his dramatic plays. Shortly after that they all went to the mess hall for a short program the campers had planned to entertain their parents. Punch and cookies were served at the close of the program. Following that, Max announced that it was time for them to start back to Summerville.

* * *

Tori did not talk as they drove away. She secured her seat belt and sat squarely in her seat, looking out the windshield at the road as she pondered what Robin had revealed to her about her mother.

"You're unusually quiet all of a sudden," Max said. "Did all those eight- and-nine-year-old girls wanting to look at you and get your autograph wear you out?"

"Absolutely not," she answered emphatically. "It was fun for me and for Robin too, most of the time."

Max shot her a concerned look. "What do you mean? Did something happen at the camp that bothered you?"

"I thought something might have upset Robin, although she handled it well. She's quite mature for her age I think."

"What was it?"

Tori hesitated, uncertain as to how to explain it to him. "Well, one of the campers asked Robin about her mother."

"About Janet?" His voice registered surprise. He shook his head, frowning. "Robin seldom talks about her mother. So what did she say?"

"That her mother was an actress in musicals and that she'd played in theaters all around the country. And then she told them that her mother was dead," Tori said solemnly, folding her hands together and pressing them into her lap. "I know it hurt Robin, and

I could have spared her that hurt if I'd only known about Janet being an actress. The confusion and the painful questions could have been avoided.'' Strain touched Tori's lips making them tremble.

''How stupid I am,'' he groaned, condemning himself as the implication of Tori's words became clear to him. ''I didn't think of that possibility.'' A look of pain etched a vulnerability into his face that was clearly evident to Tori, and she suddenly remembered the night Corinne had told her how vulnerable she was and then had added, 'in many ways Max is vulnerable too.'

''Well kids ask a lot of questions, you know. Eight- and nine-year-olds are curious. It was a mistake for you to bring me here with you under the circumstances.''

As if he sensed the tension that was building up between them over this situation, Max accelerated and made no further comments. Ahead, the mountains heaved into outlines against the dusk gray sky, and a lively wind blew a thin filament of clouds across the sky. In less than a mile the road widened. To one side there was a roadside pull-off with a cement picnic table and a Catskill Forest Preserve trash receptacle. Max swerved abruptly, swinging the car off the road to make a jolting stop in the gravelled parking lot adjacent to the picnic facilities.

''It's time I told you about Janet,'' he said gruffly.

"You didn't have to stop the car to do that, did you?" There was a questioning inflection in her voice.

Max shifted his position, moving his legs from under the steering wheel so he was facing her. "Explaining my highly erratic wife to you is not something I can do while driving." His terse words snapped the intimate stillness inside the car. "You see, I never really understood Janet, so it's not easy to explain her to someone else. She was complex as the devil, and her mood changed with the wind. She went up and down like a yo-yo," he said glumly, folding his arms across his chest.

Tori watched him in silence. Her green eyes anxious, her hands folded and pressed down in her lap.

"I guess I'd better start at the beginning though." He gave a resigned shrug. "I met Janet when I was at Columbia. She was a good-looking, uninhibited coed. She was up one day and down the next even then. Yet not to the extreme spells. Those developed later after Robin was born." He frowned. "No need to go into all that. Anyway, while we were at college she acted as if my writing plays was the greatest thing ever."

"Was she studying to be an actress then?"

"She wanted to sing and dance in musicals. She had no desire to become a serious dramatic actress. Janet called them self-centered, egotistical show-offs."

"I trust she didn't express such views to Corinne."

"Hardly. After all Corinne was her rich and famous

aunt, who was also picking up the tab for Janet's college expenses.''

''That sounds like Corinne. I would expect she helped out everyone in her family.'' The pleasant interjection about Corinne relieved some of the tension Tori was feeling hearing about Max's wife. She leaned back, resting her shoulders into the corner of the car seat and angling her body to face Max.

''I know she helped out Janet's mother after she was widowed, and saw to it that Janet got anything she wanted. Whatever Janet asked for Corinne provided, including a job for me.'' He hunched his shoulders in a deprecating shrug. ''Not that I didn't grab it up. I wasted no time in latching on to Corinne's influential coat tails. Voila! After that success came to Maxwell Branton.'' He arched one brow, adding wryly, ''Success in the theater that is, not in handling a curious problem that arose between Janet and me because of that very success.''

Tori eyed him curiously. ''You're talking in riddles.''

''Yeah, I guess I am. But it's something about Janet that I didn't understand then and I don't even now. It began the opening night of my first Broadway play. Janet refused to go to the theater with me.'' Max's face knotted in a grim expression. ''She offered no explanation. She simply said 'I won't see the play.' There was also a big theater party following the performance where we all waited for the reviews to come out. She wouldn't join me for that either.'' He heaved a sigh. ''It was such an important night for me. My own play and I'd directed the famous Corinne Howard in it. I was so angry with Janet, and so mortified that my own wife didn't care enough to be there with me.'' He paused, a pained look falling across his face. ''More than that, I was hurt. And I know I changed a little that night. Or, maybe I just grew up. At any rate I never was that young, or sensitive about myself and my plays from that night on.'' Regret colored his words, but he followed them with a shrug to confirm his older, wiser attitude. ''I even tried to think that Janet didn't come that night because she was afraid my play wouldn't be a successs. And she couldn't face that because she'd been the one who'd talked her aunt into letting me direct her in my own play.''

''Certainly that could have been a large part of it, Max,'' Tori interjected quickly, wanting to ease Max's recital of this trying night. ''Under those circumstances I can see how Janet would have been afraid to attend the opening night. She wanted to wait until your success with Corinne in your play was acknowledged by both the audience and the critics.''

''I might have believed that if Janet had seen the play some later time. She didn't. That first play of mine ran for four hundred and thirty seven performances and my wife didn't see one of them. What do you make of that?''

''I can't believe it.'' Tori looked incredulous.

"Well, it's true, and that's just the tip of the iceberg." He spoke in a calm tone, but there was a wry twist to his mouth. "Not only that first play, but any play of mine. Janet never attended a play I directed, ever. What you may find odder than that is that Janet not once in her life saw Corinne on stage." His laugh was disparaging. "This enigmatic woman who married me because I was a playwright, and who was truly obsessed with wanting me to direct Corinne in every play she was in, never stepped foot in a theater to see a one of those plays."

"Why not?" Tori asked.

"Heaven only knows. I sure don't. That first time I asked her why and she wouldn't try to explain. She just became depressed and wouldn't even talk about it. I never asked her again after that. I knew I would only upset her more if I did."

"How did Corinne feel about Janet never coming to see her in your play?" Tori asked, wanting to put all the pieces together so she'd get a clearer conception of Max's wife.

"I don't know," he answered, a look of uncertainty creeping into his expression. "Corinne never mentioned it to me. She may not have even been aware of it however, because she didn't see that much of Janet." He frowned. "I never could understand why, but Janet and Corinne were not as close as I would have expected them to be."

Confused at hearing this, Tori regarded Max quizzically for a moment. ''That's surprising. Especially because Corinne is so attached to Robin. I got the idea that Corinne spent a lot of time with Robin.''

Max nodded. ''Yes, she did. She saw Robin all the time, but never Janet. Janet had started touring with musical productions. She was away eight or twelve weeks at a time. She'd scarcely finish with one show then she'd get a part in another and be off again. From the time Robin was two, the main people in her life besides me were Corinne, Griff, and our incomparable housekeeper Audrey Rose McClary. Janet was the pretty lady who came for a visit from time to time, bringing Robin dolls, and teddy bears, and pretty little dresses with matching socks. She'd sing Robin all the songs from the musicals, do some of the dance routines, and a week or so later leave again saying 'Goodbye, remember Mommy loves you.' This was the pattern of my daughter's life. It wasn't good. It wasn't normal. Not for Robin, not for me, and I believed it wasn't normal or fulfilling for Janet. It was at this point that I took steps to change the pattern for the three of us. It didn't turn out well, I'm afraid.'' His eyes darkened with emotion as a glazed look of despair spread over his face.

Looking at him, Tori sensed that Max was burdened with some kind of guilt about his wife. Why, she wondered? Was it something he'd done? Something he'd failed to do? Whatever it might be she doubted that he'd tell her unless she asked, and she knew that she couldn't ask. Not yet. Not while sadness fell across his face, covering his features like a tragic mask.

Abruptly she shoved against the door handle, jumped quickly out of the car, then thrust the door shut behind her. Moving as rapidly as she could, she skirted the picnic table and walked into the midst of a cluster of trees whose leafy boughs interlocked over her head, shutting out the sky. All was green darkness here. She leaned against the rough bark of a tree trunk and closed her eyes.

The things Max had revealed to her were all surprising. Not at all the story of a man, his wife and his child that she might have expected to hear from him. It was hard for her to picture the odd pattern his life had taken with Janet. Yet, recalling his words, she sensed that there were some dark tiles in that mosaic that he hadn't told her about. Painful bits from the past that cut deep, leaving scars that had not yet healed.

How many minutes Tori remained lost in thought like this she didn't know. She was aware only of the high, thin hum of silence that rang in her ears. She did not hear Max open or close the car door, nor his footsteps muffled by the damp, moss covered ground as he came after her. He was behind her, not touching her. She felt his presence for the air around him was an aureole of warmth which covered her back and shoulders.

He moved behind her, his hands taking her shoulders, pulling her back so she leaned against him. His fingers moved touching the nape of her neck. Her heart was beating raggedly and she could not move, she had no desire to. She felt his breath on her skin as he kissed her neck softly.

An excruciating longing stirred achingly in her as Max turned her around to face him. She watched his eyes darken with emotion as he circled his arms around her.

''I don't know if you'll agree with me, but I know that what took place today with you and Robin and with me was positive—and it was good. I'm glad it happened. I want you to be glad too.''

Tori's eyes smiled up into his as he lowered his lips to hers. Then he was kissing her without restraint and she answered him with a yearning that sprang up from the depths of her heart.

They stood clinging to each other until they both regained a measure of composure. Finally they drew apart and stared wonderingly into each other's eyes. Tori was profoundly moved by the manifold emotions reflected in Max's face as he raised his hand, curving it caressingly to her cheek, his gaze steadfast. The silent communication between them was more explicit than words could ever be. . . .

Chapter Ten

The fast-paced comedy, *Polka Dots on a Zebra*, was the second play of the summer. It proved to be even more enthusiastically received than the acting company's opening play. Gordon Gentry had only a bit part, but his one amusing scene proved hilarious and brought the biggest laughs from the audience. This approval of his comic talent was encouraging to Gordon. Especially so because his acting experience was limited to modest parts in some of the television soaps, and he was well aware that Max had taken him into the acting group only because he was Jill's husband.

As Tori, Corinne and Griff listened to Max explain his selection for their third play of the summer, Tori was thinking about the unique quality of summer theater: a small and varied group of actors not only works together, but also lives in close association with each other. Thus the interplay of the varied personalities and temperaments affects the quality of everyone's performance on stage, as well as the emotional climate between them when they're off stage. . . .

"The title of it is *A Game of Musical Chairs.* Intriguing, huh. You remember playing musical chairs don't you, Corinne?" The four of them were having a late lunch in the dining room at the lodge before Griff headed back to New York.

"That's an old-fashioned game that went on before my time. I'm not Grandma Moses you know." Corinne hunched her dainty shoulders in disdain, using a reprimanding tone.

Her reaction seemed to amuse him. "This *cool* play was written by twenty-eight year old C. J. Duffy. There is absolutely nothing old-fashioned about it. I assure you. It's contemporary as today, fresh, clever, funny and at the same time it's both dramatic and moving. In short it's one heck of a strong play. I wish I'd written it." Max added, slapping his hand down on the table to emphasize his words.

"I thought Corinne told me you had written a fine new play, Max," Griff intervened. "I got the idea you might try it out here this summer."

Max shot a warning look at the older man, his jaw clenched, his eyes slightly narrowed. Obviously he resented Griff's interuption. "It's still in the mill," he answered brusquely. "But the play we're doing here next is this Clark Duffy one. It's a sure-fire showcase for the talents of everyone in our present company.

"In this play you're paired with Lon, Tori."

Max's mention of her name pulled her attention back to the table conversation. "With Lon," she parroted in a bemused tone.

"Lon's character is that of a man pathetically out of step with the world around him. A trusting, sensitive dreamer, hc never comes to terms with the realities of the nineties. Yours is an ill-suited romance that is funny at times, sadly touching at others."

"Combination of Tori and young Taylor, that sounds good," Griff commented. "In fact, it puts me in mind of the first time I ever saw Corinne on stage. She played opposite that intense young fellow from Britain. Whatever happened to him, by the way?"

"Jeremy Minton, you mean." Corinne inclined her head toward Griff, a pleased glint in her expressive eyes. "He went back to England and the Royal Theater. That has to have been eighteen years ago or more. Imagine you remembering a play I was in that long ago," she said, smiling softly.

Griff covered her hand where it lay on the table between them. "I remember every part you've played from then to now, both on stage and off," he said, returning her smile. "Any Corinne Hayes performance is unforgettable."

"Amen to that," Max concurred. "And wait until we all see what she does with the gem of a part she has in this play. In fact, everybody has his own brilliant moment. I'm casting Brandon with Jill as lovers whose explosive emotions erupt like a fireworks display.''

Corinne appeared to listen to Max, a benign expression on her face. When he mentioned Brandon and Jill without saying anything further, however, her eyes became alert, critical. ''This all sounds like good theater for the rest of us Max, but you've left out Gordon Gentry.'' She paused, as if waiting for Max to speak up. When he didn't, she continued. ''It's going to be a hard enough pill for Gordon to swallow, watching his wife play firey love scenes with your big male movie star. At least you could let him have his own minute of acting glory in this play.''

Tori looked at Max to see his reaction to Corrine's words. She knew Max well enough to know he'd resent casting suggestions from anyone, even Corinne.

''I've listed the roles, Corinne,'' Max said in an indulgent tone. ''I'm afraid Gordon will have to sit this one out. There's just not a part in it for him.''

''Well, it's a real shame to make him feel inadequate and a lesser talent to the rest of the company,'' she countered, a sharp edge to her voice.

''He is a lesser talent, for Pete's sake.'' Scowling, Max picked up his fork, jabbing at the food on the plate in front of him.

A short time later when the waiter wheeled the dessert cart to their table, Corinne rose to leave. ''I can't take the calories, and I've no intention of torturing myself watching the rest of you indulge.'' With a dramatic flourish she tossed her napkin down and turned away. Griff excused himself and accompanied Corinne from the dining room.

Left alone, the two of them made their selections from the tray of appealing sweets. Tori chose cheesecake, Max chocolate cream pie. Then they looked at each other and laughed conspiratorially.

''Corinne and her personal crusades. She does like to indulge in that queen-mother role of hers,'' Max scoffed making a wry face.

Tori leveled a finger at him. ''You were pretty short with her, Max.''

''If I hadn't been she'd still be at me, suggesting ten ways to recast and revise this play.'' He squared the dessert plate in front of him, eyeing the whipped cream-topped concoction, and all but smacking his lips in anticipation.

''Couldn't you add one more musical chair to the game for Gordon?''

He grimaced at her attempt to be clever. ''Don't you start on me too.''

''I'm not going to. It's just that I feel sorry for Gordon. He doesn't have too much self-confidence. That's probably because he's the only one in our group who's never played on Broadway. And of course, his wife's career far out-distances his as well. That's rough on a guy.''

"Could be rough on a marriage too. That's what Corinne identifies with, I'll bet," Max said, rubbing his hand along the side of his jaw thoughtfully. "She knows how readily an ambitious actress will discard an actor husband whose acting career doesn't get off the ground."

Tori registered disbelief. "You're not telling me that Corinne did anything like that."

"I was told she did exactly that."

Tori leaned across the table, her eyes alight with curiosity. "Who told you?"

"Janet did. She claimed that her Aunt Corinne was the member of the family who would allow absolutely nothing to stand in the way of her career. The way she put it was that Corinne shed all the excess baggage that cluttered her life. Which she said included a no-good actor husband."

Tori shook her head. "That's hard to believe."

"Sure it is now. But how can you or I know what Corinne was like at the beginning of her career. That was some thirty years ago, you know."

Still shaking her head, Tori narrowed her eyes at Max questioningly. "Why is it that we've never read that she was once married in any of the newspaper and magazine articles that have been written about her acting career? Good heavens, Max. A discarded husband is the kind of thing that gives the media a hey-day."

"Everybody has something in their past they want

to keep hidden. My guess is that Corinne managed to closet her skeletons more successfully than some of the rest of us.'' Max looked away from her as he spoke, glancing out the window, his eyes fixed on a remote stare. The light fell across part of his face, throwing into relief the stark angle of his cheekbone and jaw.

Tori was strangely jarred by this. He had withdrawn from her as completely as if he had stood up and left the table. It was not Corinne's skeletons so much as his own that he was thinking about, and she knew it. Her hand crept to her throat and anger rose inside her making her want to lash out at him and ask how much more of his past was he hiding from her? She pulled the unspoken words down and they broke like a wet aspirin tablet in her throat, choking her and filling her mouth with a sharp, bitter taste.

Finally she broke the silence. ''It's late. Didn't you tell everybody to meet at the playhouse at three o'clock?''

Max turned his head sharply and blinked his eyes as if he needed to change their focus. The following moment he pushed his shirt cuff off his wrist and inspected his watch. ''It's only two-thirty. I've time for another cup of coffee,'' he answered, fingering his watch, then adjusting the strap to center the watch in a slightly different place on his wrist.

She watched his movements in sad fascination. What bothers him, she wondered? Does he find his past immutable? Is it that he can't escape something he did and his guilt keeps coming back to slap him in the face. He's acting, she thought. He's using that watch as a prop and directing himself through some cathartic scene.

"I'm going to my room for something," she muttered, rising quickly from the table. "I'll join you at the playhouse at three." Not intending to give Max a chance to object, or try to detain her, she immediately walked away, holding herself straight and moving with her characteristic grace. At the doorway she did not look back. She had no wish to see Max's face, watch him suffer as he crawled back over the shards of shattered illusions that had been his marriage to Janet.

"Our third production is to be a brilliant new play, *A Game of Musical Chairs,*" Max announced when the members of the company had all gathered at the theater. "It has never been performed before, so we'll be introducing it. It has five balanced roles. Each part with a jewel-bright quality of its own." There was a flicker of warning light in Max's eyes, indicating that neither Corinne nor anyone else should interrupt with a comment. "There are two pairs of lovers. One played by Tori and Lon, the other by Jill and Brandon."

There was a moment of stillness and then Corinne spoke out. "And I'm the sometimes evil, sometimes righteous character who manipulates the chairs and the music in this game."

Another second of hushed quiet followed Corinne's announcement. Tori saw Jill's brows arch and her questioning eyes seek out those of her husband. Max apparently noticed this too. He cleared his throat noisily. "This play has only a cast of five as I've said. So I'm expecting Gordon to act as spokesman for the theater company. Opening night he'll give some background information about *A Game of Musical Chairs* and about the author, C. J. Duffy. Now Clark Duffy and I are friends," he added with a sly smile. "So I've prevailed on him to come over from Poughkeepsie and join us for as many performances as he will. Gordon will be the one to bring Clark out on stage and introduce him to our audiences."

"Not exactly a plum Max is giving Gordon, but it's a saving grace," Corinne muttered under her breath. She was sitting beside Tori, and fortunately the two of them were sufficiently separated from Jill and Gordon that Corinne's remarks couldn't be overheard.

Max immediately passed out the play books to the five in the cast. There was high color in Gordon's face as he stood to one side, waiting for Jill to get her script. The Gentrys then were the first to leave the playhouse. Corinne did not linger either.

Lon came over to Tori. "I'd like to run lines with you before the first rehearsal," he said.

"Fine. Let's do that."

"I'm really eager to read through this play." He fingered the edges of his play book as he said this. "I know a litte about the author. I've read both of the novels he's written. He's a writer with something to say all right. I'm betting this play of his is as good as his books.'' Lon burst out with this in that intense, enthusiastic way he had whenever he spoke of anything to do with acting or the theater.

Tori smiled, thinking how young and eager he was, seeming younger in some ways even than his twenty-one or two years. ''Max talks as if it's a brilliant play that has everything, so let's both read it and then get together like you suggested.''

''Could we do it tomorrow? Is that too soon?''

Tori laughed. ''The sooner the better. Knowing Max he'll expect us to be up on our lines in twenty-four hours. You know that.''

''Would you have lunch with me tomorrow then? We could work together afterwards.''

''O.K., it's a date,'' she said.

''Hey, don't make a date for tonight Tori,'' Max warned, approaching the two of them. ''Brandon just now told me there's a band and one of the up-and-coming singing groups appearing at the dance pavilion at the upper end of the lake. I thought following the performance tonight we'd check it out.''

''Everybody will want to hear that,'' Tori said, prompting Max to be inclusive. ''After all it is Saturday night and the final performance of *Polka Dots on a Zebra*. We'll all want to party a little.''

''Sure thing.'' Max agreed, clapping Lon on his

shoulder. "Brandon and I will both take our cars. There's plenty of room for all."

"Thanks, but don't count on me tonight." Lon took a step back from Tori. "I'm not much on dancing, and I'm anxious to read the new play before tomorrow." There was a look of tension in his lean face, and a silver sheen grayed his blue eyes. It struck Tori that there was a brooding loneliness inside Lon Taylor. She wondered what caused it.

The pavilion was a green-painted wooden structure built close to the rim of the lake. The edges and peak of the roof were outlined with strings of white lights. Inside the lights were dim and all of a soft yellow color which was intended to give the dancers the illusion of dancing beneath moonlight.

Tori and Max sat down at a table on a raised tier against the lakeside wall of the building. Through the open windows they could see a lopsided moon in the jet night heaven. Scattered about were patches of stars and they appeared like a wash of diamonds against the black velvet sky.

"Glad we came?" Max asked as they sat drinking beer from thick round glasses and eating pretzels.

Tori nodded. "Yeah, I like this. It reminds me of one of those old summer places at Atlantic City."

"Sort of," he agreed. This place is a shade more rustic though. It could also do with a fresh coat of paint."

"No. Its antiquity is what gives it a sort of Rip Van

Winkle charm. This is in the Sleepy Hollow country Irving wrote about, you know.''

''I know that. I took American Lit 101 same as you did. But some guy who sleeps for twenty years doesn't impress me as much as he does you obviously.'' He laughed. ''Anyway I didn't come here to study the architecture. I had a better reason than that.''

''I'll bet you did, and I can guess what your reason was.'' She glanced around at the noisy people at tables near theirs. ''You wanted to ogle the bevy of college girls who have summer jobs here in the Catskills and wear cut off jeans and halter tops,'' she said, a glint of laughter in her teasing eyes.

''That was my second reason,'' he countered, giving her a wicked grin.

''What was your first?''

''That's easy. You see I've never danced with you, and I very much wanted to.'' His grin was gone and his caressing eyes were humorous and tender.

''You're right. We never have danced together.''

Max stood up and pulled her to her feet. ''Let's remedy that right now.''

Hand in hand they made their way through the crowd to an empty area at one corner of the dance floor. Max circled his arm around her waist and adeptly led her with smooth gliding steps into the rhythm of the music. Tori followed Max's lead and they danced well together.

''You dance with the same harmony of movement

as when you walk.'' Max complimented her at the beginning. After that they simply danced.

When the music changed, becoming louder and faster, they danced on to the crazy, wild beat. The rhythm built and they were two bodies answering its challenge, moving together in response to it. A variety of tempos—fast, moderate and slow—followed as the band played on and on. Max and Tori never left the floor. They danced the other dancers out of the room and the music into silence.

Tori shivered as they finally left the pavilion for the pre-dawn air felt glass sharp and cold coming off the lake. A shredded morning mist hung like spiders' webs in the trees. Max held her close in the curve of his arm as they walked to his car.

''I wish I could have known you in college, Tori. You're the one with whom I should have shared all the fun things.''

''I would have liked that,'' she answered, smiling up at him.

They drove back to Summerville sitting close together, sharing the silence as they had shared the music. It had been a romantic night. Max had said that he wished they'd known each other earlier, in his youthful college days. Wished that she'd been the one he'd shared all the fun with, the dancing, the music, shows and football games, all the wonderful, carefree things young couples do. It was the nearest Max had come to saying—if only he'd met her first. Before

Janet—before Robin—before whatever the nameless barriers were that still stood between them. If only, she thought, suppressing a sigh. If only that could have been. . . .

Chapter Eleven

T ori stirred into wakefulness reluctantly. It took her sleep-fogged senses several seconds to realize the repeating sound throbbing in her ears was the telephone. Because the bed was secluded in an alcove, she had to get up to reach the phone which sat on the lamp table between the pair of upholstered chairs at the other end of her room. She slowly eased her legs over the side of the bed and forced herself to sit up. Awake enough now to be aware that the phone had sounded numerous times, she scurried across the rug in her bare feet and grabbed up the receiver.

"Hello," she said in a breathy voice.

"Tori, I'm downstairs waiting for you." It was Lon sounding anxious and concerned. "You haven't forgotten you promised to have lunch with me and run through our lines, have you?''

''Oh my gosh! What time is it anyway?''

''It's twelve. I thought we decided to meet at eleven thirty and take in the Sunday brunch buffet.''

''I'm sorry, Lon,'' she apologized. ''I was out dancing very late. I'm afraid I just woke up.'' She paused, making negative shuddering sounds under her breath. ''Worse yet, you're going to want to kill me. I haven't even read the play. I haven't had time.''

There was silence from his end and she sensed his disappointment, suspecting he was pretty irritated with her as well.

''Look, I know what we could do. I'll get dressed as fast as I can. While I'm doing that, you go through the buffet line and fill two plates. Bring them up here to my room and we'll eat and you can tell me about the play and our parts. We'll not be bothered with other people and noise here by ourselves, and we can run our lines more comfortably in my lounge chairs than over in those hard seats at the playhouse.'' Tori talked fast and with a burst of enthusiasm in an effort to regain Lon's good graces.

The new arrangements made, Tori dashed into the bathroom, ducking under the shower for a few brief minutes. Then she dressed rapidly in jeans and a light blue shirt that had a white collar and roll up sleeves fastened back with buttoned tabs. As soon as she had her hair combed, she added a touch of blusher to her cheeks and a rose gloss to her lips. She opened the door leaving it ajar for Lon before disappearing into the alcove to make her bed. She was tucking the blue and white toile spread over the pillow when Lon came in with their food.

Lon's generous mouth formed a wide grin when she came quickly to greet him. With a wave of her hand she directed Lon to carry the tray over to the large square lamp table. Preceding him, she set the lamp off, clearing the table top for them to eat on.

"I didn't know exactly what you like so I brought some of everything," he said as she took the plates of food and the serving pot of coffee from the tray, arranging them with the silver on the table.

"I can see that." She angled her head at him, laughing. "I'm wondering what you left for those eating in the dining room."

"Don't worry. That's some spread they lay out on Sunday."

While they ate, Lon told Tori about the play, describing in detail the characters the two of them would be playing. He was explicit, too, in giving her a rundown as to exactly what their scenes together were like. Listening to him, Tori got the feeling that Lon identified himself in a major degree to the role he was taking.

"You sound as if you've a strong grasp on your character already."

"I understand him," Lon said, a look of sadness

reflecting in his silver-blue eyes. "He's a misfit. One of the lonesome breed who lives in his illusions because he can't face realities." He was intently serious, and there was such a look of pain marking his lean face that Tori felt it too and had to look away.

Sometime later, after Tori and Lon had read through their scenes several times, Tori suggested that they had worked enough and had earned the right to spend the remainder of the afternoon relaxing and having a good time.

"It's Sunday and our director does give us Sundays off you know," she said, stretching her arms over her head and yawning. "I for one am ready to get out of this room. Let's you and I go find something fun to do around here."

"That suits me. How'd you like to take one of the hiking trails up the mountain behind the lodge?" he asked, rolling his playbook and sticking it in his pocket.

"Sounds interesting." She jumped up from her chair and held out her hand to him. "Let's go. I have to be here at seven to meet Max when he get's back from his daughter's camp, but for the rest of the day I'm all yours."

"I could only wish that were true," he muttered under his breath.

"What did you say?" she asked, slanting her eyes curiously.

"Nothing that I'll repeat. You wouldn't understand, and I can't explain."

Tori stared at him, baffled by his obscure words. "Look, if there's something wrong—"

"Hey, I'm sorry," he interrupted her. "There's nothing wrong, nothing at all. I'm just one of those weird actors that can't step in and out of a part just like that." He snapped his fingers. "I guess I haven't gotten away from the brooding, misfit guy of this play yet."

"Well for heaven's sake shed that part. I've a strong preference for the real Lon Taylor." She spoke lightly, but she certainly meant what she'd said. She admired Lon's extraordinary talent and sensitivity. However, she hoped she wasn't going to discover that he had a moody temperament to go with it.

Everyone in the cast was excited about *A Game of Musical Chairs*. Max told them at rehearsal that the interest was running high on the play because it was the first production of Clark Duffy's first play. Already recognized for his best-selling novels he was expected to gain further laurels now as a playwright. "I shouldn't be surprised if we get some media people, drama critics and the like tomorrow night for the opening. So let's give it everything we've got!"

It was the final rehearsal and Max kept them late. He went over some scenes time and time again, buffing and polishing the skill of each of their performances to a superlative luster. When they were finally finished, Max laid a restraining hand on Tori's arm as the others left.

''Wait while I lock up here. Then I'll walk with you back to the lodge.''

She nodded and then began rubbing the back of her neck to see if she could unwind a bit. She felt like a coiled spring, for doing a tensely emotional play like this one gave her a feeling of being electrically charged and unable to turn off the current. As she flexed her shoulders she watched Max switching off the stage lights, and then the two of them walked down the aisle together. When Max had secured the doors they left the theater.

Outside, the summer night was cool. Stars clustered here and ranged there against the soft blackness of the sky. ''It's far too nice a night to end right now,'' Max said as they climbed the steps to the lodge. ''What do you say we go sit close together there in the shadows down at the end of the veranda.''

''If that's what you'd like to do.''

Some private emotion glistened in his eyes. ''It's one of the things. Shall I list the others?'' he asked, with a lazy deepening of his voice.

''No!'' She silenced him emphatically.

Max laughed, and his laughter was a rich resonant sound born deep in his throat.

''And stop laughing. You're embarrassing me.''

''At least I took your mind off the play and Lon's

mesmerizing acting talents,'' Max declared, gently shoving her toward the darkened end of the porch.

''What made you say that about Lon and the play?'' Tori asked him. Max didn't answer and she was about to rephrase her question and ask him again.

''Because, like you and probably everyone else in our company, I'm trying to get a hold on this elusive quality in Lon's acting that makes his performance so profoundly moving,'' Max said finally.

''He's gifted with talent that exceeds the rest of us. I think that's most of it. Then too, he's intensely absorbed in this role. Don't you get the idea that he identifies himself to some degree with his character?''

''That's a lot of it, but it's not all. You're also a part of it, Tori.''

''Me?'' She raised a curious eyebrow. ''I don't see how.''

Max draped his arm across the back of the glider not far from her shoulder. ''Don't you know that the two of you were hypnotic together? You held everybody spellbound in that final scene tonight. You and Lon were so caught up in the vortex of passion and heartbreak that the performance was stunning. In fact, to me it went beyond performing.''

Tori's head snapped around as she stared at him. ''What do you mean?''

''I honestly believe that illusion has become reality for Lon in this one. He sees himself emotionally involved with you in and out of this play.''

Tori scowled at him. "That's idiotic nonsense," she said sharply. "More than that it's absurd for you to base all this on the fact that Lon's skilled acting moved us all to tears tonight. Isn't that exactly the reaction you want from the audiences who see *A Game of Musical Chairs?*"

She could feel the tension now between them, hanging in the air like a curtain of gauze. Why had Max brought this up in the first place? He wouldn't possibly think that she would encourage Lon in any kind of relationship. "Listen to me, Max. You've got a fine play opening tomorrow night. A play that you've cast and directed to perfection. Don't mess with that." Her voice rose in anger. "And don't you dare make me uneasy about acting with Lon. His great portrayal adds luster to my role. Just be grateful for that. I certainly am."

There was a tightening of the lines that ran from Max's nostrils to the corners of his mouth. "Right. We'll leave it at that."

Tori took a deep steadying breath. "Peace," she said, managing a small conciliatory smile.

"Peace," he responded without changing his expression.

They had been on the verge of an argument that neither of them wanted. Tori recognized the effort Max was making to avoid conflict between them.

The strongly etched lines at the edge of Max's mouth had eased somewhat, but his eyes remained shadowed and intent. It was obvious that he had something else on his mind, and it was bothering him as much or more than what he'd brought up regarding Lon. She wondered if he were going to broach it with her now.

''I was just listening to that wind that's come up and is blowing and soughing through the pines.'' He shrugged. ''It's like my grumblings, just sound and fury meaning nothing.'' He gave her an apologetic smile.

''Here in the Catskills 'nothing' could be a rain storm moving down from the mountains,'' she countered.

Max was quick to agree with her, because at that very minute the rain began falling through the trees with a whispering sound.

Wherever there is magic and make-believe and an audience—there is theater. All the elements combined that opening night in the playhouse at Summerville. The audience moved in, taking programs and finding seats. And when the footlights went on, beaming toward the actors on stage, the make-believe and the magic began. Thereafter, minute by minute, the audience was swept into the magnetic field of certainty that *A Game of Musical Chairs* was theater at its best.

All of this was true for every performance first to last. Clark Duffy was there every night, and as Max had predicted the play had rave reviews from the numerous critics and theater publications columnists who came to view this first production of the Duffy play.

The morning after the final performance Tori got a call from her agent.

"I've got some great news for you, Tori." Jayson's voice held even more than his usual enthusiasm. "A television casting director saw you in that play you've just done and they want you for the six-hour miniseries of the novel *Wheat Lands*. What do you say about that?"

"Wow! You know I've been hoping for a big miniseries and *Wheat Lands* was a major book."

"You're right. I'd bet the TV adaptation will rank up there right along with *Lonesome Dove*."

Tori's voice crescendoed with elation. "Tell me— tell me quick. What part do they want me for?"

"Cassie, the troubled young farmer's wife."

"Oooh, that's fantastic. She was a really pivotal character in the book. Before she gets killed off in a tornado, that is."

Jayson laughed. "Then you won't mind dying during the fourth hour of the show, I guess."

"You just get it in my contract that I die on camera. A dramatic death scene is worth more than getting your name first on the credits," she countered with a bright laugh.

"Okay, you prarie Camile, let's get back to business for a minute. They're gonna film *Wheat Lands* in Kansas, starting the middle of August. I told them you'd be in summer theater until the end of August. That's no problem as long as you get there immediately after you close in Summerville.''

''Fine. I'll be on the first plane out to the sunflower state the morning after our fourth play closes. You assure them of that,'' she said, underlining her words emphatically. ''And thanks, Jayson. You're the best.''

Chapter Twelve

Tori glanced quickly at her watch as soon as she hung up the phone. She'd really have to make a run for it if she was going to get to the playhouse on time. Max had called a meeting of the company for ten-thirty. That only gave her five minutes to get out of her room, down the stairs and out of the lodge onto the path to the theater.

As it turned out she made it exactly to the minute. A split second later Max came striding down the aisle to join the group.

"Thank you all for being prompt. You know how I like to get things going on time," he said with a quick, self-mocking smile. "And seeing we're all here I'll get right to the point and tell you what plans I've made for us for these last few weeks at the playhouse.'' Max raised his voice just enough to control their attention, rather like the captain of the ship saying *now here this*. ''As some of you probably know my daughter, Robin, has been at a summer camp near here. Her camp is out today, and right after we finish this meeting I'm driving over to get her and bring her back here. She'll spend the time here with me while we do our last summer play.''

''Oh, that's wonderful,'' Corinne said. ''I was hoping to have some time with her.''

''Robin will enjoy herself here too. That's going to be fun for both of you,'' Tori whispered to Corinne.

''And it'll give you a chance to get to know her really well,'' Corinne whispered back. ''I'm so glad for that.''

''Ladies, we're not really here to talk about my daughter you know,'' Max admonished them gently. ''To get back to business at hand. It was my original intention to test a new play of mine here this summer. This latest work of mine, entitled *All the Tomorrows*, is what I want to take to Broadway next season. If I do say so myself, it's the best play I've ever written, possibly the best I'll ever write.''

Brandon's face began to light up, and at the same time Lon sat forward eagerly in his seat. Corinne slanted her eyes quizzically, her forehead faintly creased. ''You've changed your mind?'' Her crystal clear voice rose in a questioning inflection.

Max nodded solemnly. ''I'm going to hold up on it

and go to a frothy bit of light comedy for our final play here.''

''Why?'' Corinne voiced the question the rest of them hesitated to ask. ''Certainly you've got enough talent here for *All the Tomorrows*. Besides, you told me you wanted to get the jump on other new productions for next season by testing audience reaction here this summer.''

''Corinne,'' Max's voice was constrained as he spoke in a placating voice. ''You are the star of my new play, but I'm its director. Let's just say I've changed my mind about tackling it here. My decision has nothing to do with any lack of talent. Heaven knows there's an abundance for me to choose from, with all of you.'' He took them all in with a smile and a sweeping glance. ''I've simply decided there would be too much stress and strain to initiating my new play. With Robin here with me, I want to have time to be a father as well as a director. It's easier for all of us this way. Believe me we'll all welcome the light fun and easy time we'll have doing *Love Is a Soap Bubble*. That is what our last summer offering will be.'' He paused long enough to check his wrist watch. ''Well that seems to be it for now. We'll discuss the roles and I'll have playbooks for you tonight when I get back with my daughter.'' He stood up and took a step toward where Tori was sitting. ''Come along with me. I need to talk to you before I leave for the camp,'' he said, holding out his hand to her.

Corinne's intent gaze had remained on Max throughout the explanatory monologue he'd offered all of them. Now she shrugged her petite shoulders and turned to talk to Jill and Gordon in a reserved voice that excluded Max and Tori. She did not look up to see when they left the theater, but Tori noticed the signs that indicated how much Corinne had been affected by Max's announcement. Corinne's expressive hands had touched each individual pearl along one side of the long strand she was wearing in the manner of someone fingering the beads of a rosary. And now as she inclined her auburn head close to Jill's, talking intently to her, she nervously wrapped the lower end of her strand of pearls around her index finger.

"You've upset Corinne," Tori told Max as they walked away from the playhouse.

"Oh, she's just irritated with me because I changed my plans without discussing it first with her."

"Why didn't you?"

Max rammed his hands into his pockets and scowled at her. "Because it's my play, Tori. I spent two years writing it, and to tell you the truth, I believe it could be the most important thing I've done in the theater. So I intend to be certain I put it into performance at the right time and under all the right circumstances." He quickened his steps. "Neither the time nor the circumstances are good for me now. Corinne will realize that too, once she takes the time to think it through."

Tori quickened her steps to keep up with him. "Do we have to walk this fast?" She put her hand on his arm to slow his pace.

He took his hands out of his pockets and put one arm around her waist. "I'll slow down if we'll change the subject and talk about a special all-day event where I want to take you and Robin tomorrow."

A look of interest quickened on her face. "Sounds intriguing. Let's do talk about that," she said, with a quick smile. "What sort of event is it? And where is it?"

"Ever hear of a German Alps Festival?"

"No I can't say I have." She glanced up at him quizzically. "But I hardly think you'll be taking us all the way to the Bavarian Alps tomorrow. Not me anyway, because I don't have a passport."

"Aren't you the witty one," he said, with a wry grimace. "In this case, however, the setting for the festival is a place called Hunter Village and the mountains are the Catskills. And you might be interested in hearing what Robin answered when I asked her what she thought of asking you to come along to Hunter Village with us. 'Super neat idea, Daddy,' she said. And in case you're not up on the current pre-teen lingo, *super neat* is pretty terrific. Why, that's even better than *cool*." Laughing, Max hugged her waist.

Walking closely together like this, Tori had a feeling of warmth, a warmth that began to course through her and quicken her heartbeats. How glad she was that

Max and Robin wanted her to go with them tomorrow. What a *super neat* feeling she had about it. Really super neat! She looked at Max and joined her laughter with his as they walked on.

The following day, before it was even light, Tori got up and with soundless steps went out on the deck off her room. The chill that precedes dawn raised prickles on her arms. The light wind shook the trees and rustled through the pines, carrying the scent of pine resin. It was a clean, refreshing smell and Tori inhaled it deeply. Dawn began softly with light cascades of amethyst light, then scarlet sprayed upward from the rim of the earth scattering into shreds of lavender and pink. The beauty of it stung her eyes and she was filled with the kind of emotion that comes through the heart into the throat. She held her breath for a moment, thinking about the day that lay ahead with Max and Robin.

Several minutes later she headed back inside to dress. As soon as she had showered, she put on jeans and a multi colored madras shirt. She tucked a scarf in the pocket of her denim jacket, as Max had informed her there was a chairlift skyride on the mountain at Hunter Village that ascended to an elevation of thirty-two hundred feet and offered a panoramic view of the surrounding countryside. Robin wouldn't want to miss that, and if it were windy they'd both need to tie their hair back.

Thinking of this, Tori found a second and somewhat

wider silk square. This one designed in shades of blue that would be pretty for Robin with her blue eyes.

Considering Robin's swinging mane of hair and owlish eyes Tori smiled, recalling last night when Max came back from the camp with Robin.

Tori had been eating dinner at a table with Corinne, Brandon and Lon. When Corinne saw Max and Robin entering the dining room she left the table, hurrying toward the slender girl clad in faded jeans. Robin's hands and wrists emerged from folded back, blue denim shirt cuffs, looking long boned and as tanned as her slightly freckled face. At the sight of her aunt, Robin's eyes sparkled with joy, and her mouth spread wide as she grinned like a happy jack-o-lantern. Robin literally catapulted herself into Corinne's welcoming embrace.

In another month Robin would be ten. She was already about as tall as her petite aunt. With her face pressed close to Corinne's cheek they looked alike in height, and they both had the same auburn hair.

That morning as Max drove Tori and Robin to the mountain resort village for the festival, Robin had her long straight hair pulled back from her face in a neat pony tail, which she'd secured with a wide rubber band. Tori noticed that she had a two-inch long scar above her left temple that had not been revealed when she wore her hair falling loosely forward over her face. Tori started to ask Robin how she got the scar, but instantly thought better of it. Instead, she complimented her. "I like your hair in a pony tail. You look very pretty."

Robin smiled, making little shadows on her cheeks that were almost like dimples. "Thank you. It was Aunt Corinne's idea. She said I should wear it like this until we get back home, and then I should ask Daddy to let me get my hair cut with bangs. Bangs would hide my scar," she said, raising her right hand to her forehead and smoothing the small-ridged area with the tips of her fingers.

"Leave it to Corinne to come up with all the answers," Max said with a tolerant smile.

Now that the scar had been mentioned, Tori couldn't resist asking about it. "What happened to you Robin? How did you hurt your head like that?"

"Oh I didn't do it, my mommy did."

"You mean you and your mother were in an accident?"

"No, Mommy was having one of her bad spells. She pushed me and I fell," Robin stated matter-of-factly. "She didn't know she'd hurt me, I guess. 'Cause she left and didn't come with Daddy and me when I got the stitches put in." She explained this with a stoic candor that totally confounded Tori.

"That's history now," Max chimed in sharply. He immediately accelerated, making it clear that the subject of Robin's scar was not to be pursued further.

It was only a short drive to Hunter Village. They arrived before ten o'clock and there was already a festive gaiety to the place. The rich smell of newly baked bread mixed with the spicy odors of German sausages and mellow cheese permeated the air as the three of them walked among the crowded stalls. Besides the displays of tasty German and Austrian food there were booths that held all sorts of arts and crafts from the Alpine countries.

Robin darted here and there asking questions of the Tyrolean-costumed shopkeepers. At a larger booth which had wood carvings, decorated wooden boxes and Black Forest cuckoo clocks, she waited for Max and Tori to catch up with her.

"I've got money left over from camp, Daddy, so I want to buy Grandma one of these boxes. I can't decide though whether she'd like round-, square- or heart-shaped." She pulled her father over in front of the display of prettily designed boxes.

"That's too momentous a decision for a mere man," Max declared, as soon as he'd given a cursory look at the selection before him. "Let Tori help you with it while I get a good German steel pocket knife for your Granddad at that stall across the street." Max indicated a shop opposite from where they stood. Before he left the two of them he took a twenty-dollar bill from his money clip, tucking it into the pocket of Robin's denim jacket. "In case you run short," he said with a smile.

Robin didn't seem to mind that her father refused to offer an opinion on the boxes. She turned imme-

diately to Tori. "Which one do you think my grand-
mother would like?"

"Depends on what you think she will use it for,"
Tori answered, picking up a medium-sized rectangular
box from the display. "This would be good for recipe
cards or even letters and bills. The smaller round or
heart-shaped ones would be nice for jewelry." She put
back the one she was holding and fingered the lid of
a round box decorated in red, green and white.

Robin watched her thoughtfully. "I hadn't stopped
to think of what Gran might put in it." She appeared
pleased by the attention Tori was giving her selection
of a gift. Robin examined all the boxes a few minutes
longer. Then with an excited bob of her head, she
chose one of the larger boxes and handed it to the
shopkeeper. "I'd like this one, please."

Tori turned her attention to the clocks while Robin
completed her purchase. "Cuckoo clocks fascinate me
somehow," she commented when Robin sidled over
to where she stood. "How about you? Would you like
one of these smaller ones for your room?"

"There pretty cool, all right. And I guess one would
be okay in the room where I sleep when I go visit
Gran and Grandpa. But not where Daddy and I live."
She shrugged, gazing soberly at Tori. "If you've seen
our apartment you'd know that Daddy wouldn't like a
clock with a bird coming out of it every hour."

Tori burst out laughing. How right Robin was. Time
conscious as Max was, precision clocks with radial

dials were his style. He would never go for something as quaint and provincial as an Old World time piece from Germany's Black Forest.

As if she could read Tori's thoughts, Robin began to laugh too, and the two of them had their heads together shaking with mirth until Robin caught sight of her father recrossing the street to join them.

Max took hold of both Tori's arm and Robin's, spiriting them away from the cuckoo clocks and on down the street to the next shopping stall.

For once Max didn't seem to be in a hurry about anything. The three of them continued wandering among the booths at a leisurely pace until they'd seen everything. Then Max took them off to take the famed mountain skyride.

As Tori had suspected, there was a strong breeze blowing in the open area around the chairlift. Before stepping up to take her place in the waiting line, she tied her silk scarf around her head peasant style, knotting it under her chin. When she offered the blue scarf she'd brought to Robin, the young girl accepted it gratefully, immediately covering her head with it in the exact same manner as Tori. At this point Max designated the order that they would take the lift: Tori in the first chair, Robin the second and Max in the third.

Once Tori was securely anchored in her chair, she relaxed and took a deep breath of the pine-scented air. It felt good to be sitting down after all the walking they'd done. She was looking forward to experiencing the scenic vistas of the surrounding Catskills. When the climb began she saw the white skeins of waterfalls flowing down the sides of nearby mountains. She heard the sound of the rushing water below her as the chair lifted higher. When she gazed overhead into the cloud-laced sky, she caught sight of a long-winged hawk, soaring with its wings horizontal, its white head and tail a vivid contrast to its dark brown, feathered body.

The slightly rocking motion of Tori's chair was like that of a recently deserted park swing that still echoed a free swaying action. She glanced at Robin swinging in like manner directly below her, then at Max in the space further down. Mesmerized by the gentle rocking movement of Max's chair, she began to wonder if she would ever understand Max and the bits and pieces of his life that still remained shut away from her. Was Robin the key that unlocked the door? If Robin were the key then perhaps that explained why Max planned this day together at the festival. Certainly a happy rapport was developing between the three of them.

Robin glowed with enthusiasm when they had completed the sky ride and returned to the midst of the festivities to have their dinner. The crowd had swelled as the evening's entertainment got underway. Now voices rose in a surf of sound. There was a group of accordionists in Bavarian costumes playing music for dancing in the street. And where sidewalk tables had been set up outside a cafe, a chorus of singers were singing German drinking songs while pretty waitresses in red dirndl dresses dispensed steins of aromatic beer to the customers.

Max found them an empty table and soon they were eating famed Westphalian stew and caraway seed dumplings. When it came time for dessert Max and Robin opted for the Black Forest cherry torte. Tori chose Bavarian cream strudel.

"Every kind of German pastry is so rich it's sinful," she declared, as she tasted her cream and raisin-filled concoction. "I'm trying to convince myself that this isn't as fattening as your torte. At least it doesn't have the chocolate, almonds and whipped cream." She wrinkled her nose in mock horror. "If I'd had that I'd risk being thrown out of the cast of our last summer play." She laughed. "My director can't abide fat leading ladies."

Max's laughing eyes met Robin's. "She's right, I can't. But to keep a certain actress of mine from becoming fat on Bavarian strudel, I guess we could make her jog from here back to the car," he said, winking at his daughter.

"No way." Tori protested loudly. "I'll do push-ups in the morning, but for tonight nothing more energetic than a slow walk to the car and leisurely drive home."

That sounds good to me, too, Daddy." Robin said, devouring her last bite of chocolate and whipped cream. "It's been a super neat day. I'm so full and so tired I just want to go to sleep on the back seat like I used to do when I was little. You remember when Mommy would be gone all those times and you and I would drive to Vermont to visit at Gran's.''

Max expelled an audible breath, looking at his daughter with grave eyes. ''I remember those times very well, Honey,'' he said. Then he looked beyond Robin, and his eyes were glazed and he appeared lost in thought.

It was as if Max had turned inward, looking back down the corridor of time, Tori thought. Watching him, Tori had a feeling that he wasn't happy with what he saw as he remembered those yesterdays that Robin had reminded him of.

Chapter Thirteen

The mountains loomed tall and dark, the farther peaks shadowy in the distance against the pale night sky. In the back seat of the car Robin had fallen asleep exactly as she'd planned. In the front seat Tori listened to the soft strains of music coming from the car radio. Absently, she studied Max's hands on the leather-wrapped steering wheel, his long fingers, square nails, the thread of a scar near his thumb. She suppressed an urge to reach out, touch his hand, ask how he got the scar.

Instead, she closed her eyes and let the music lead her thoughts wherever they wished to go. She wondered what Max was thinking about. Was he remembering the past? searching, as she was, for answers—for solutions? They sat, each in their own silence, as separate as a pair of book ends on a library shelf.

After a while, Max took his hand off the steering wheel and rested it on the seat between them. When he did this, Tori reached out and slipped her hand beneath his. Max's hand felt cold. He let it lie in hers without moving for only a second before he laced his fingers between hers. The black ribbon of road hissed beneath the car wheels. Max gave her hand a reassuring squeeze. "I thought there for a minute that you'd gone to sleep on me like Robin has."

Tori shook her head. "I didn't want to talk for fear of waking her, so I was listening to the radio."

"Don't have to worry about that daughter of mine. She'll sleep soundly as long as the car is moving. I've driven many a mile with her curled up on the front seat beside me. She never stirred until the car stopped." He slowed his speed, glancing over his shoulder into the back seat. He chuckled, adding, "That was before she grew willowy and long-legged, however. Now she has to draw her knees up some to even fit in the whole back seat."

"How old was she back then?"

"Little over two. You see, about the time Robin was a year and a half old, Janet got a part in the road company of *A Chorus Line.* She was gone eight to ten weeks at a time, and this meant that Audrey Rose took over the care of Robin. Bless her warm Irish heart, I don't know how we'd have ever gotten along without her. She'd raised four children of her own and she watched over Robin like a mother hen with a chick.'' His smile indicated this was a fond memory to him. ''However, I wanted Robin's early childhood to include more family than just me and a sometimes glimpse of Janet, so at least one weekend a month I'd drive up to Vermont with her and let my folks have their turn at nurturing and spoiling their only grandchild.'' He chuckled. ''They *did spoil* her, let me tell you!''

''Of course, they did. That's what grandparents are for. Everybody knows that,'' she teased.

There was a lull in their conversation as Max eased the accelerator, slowing the car for a sweeping curve in the road. Tori waited until he had regained travel speed on the straight stretch of road beyond the curve before bringing up the question which had been needling her mind throughout this entire day. '

''Maybe you'd rather I didn't ask, but something came up this morning with Robin that I can't get off my mind.''

''You mean there's more to that business about my taking you to the camp to see Robin.''

''No, not that. It's about this morning in the car. You know, when Robin was talking about Corinne saying she should get her hair cut and have bangs.''

Max shot her a puzzled glance. ''What about it?''

Tori shifted nervously in her seat. ''Well I—,'' she hesitated and cleared her throat, ''I hoped you'd tell me what happened. Exactly how did Robin get that scar?''

Max's tense expression grew even more clenched. Several moments passed and then with what seemed like a great effort of will on his part, his face became flat again, like a piece of crumpled paper that's been smoothed out. ''I never thought I could tell anyone about it. But you've asked, and I'll tell you. Only I'll warn you it was a bad scene, really bad. And there was no happy ending,'' he said morosely.

''When was this, Max?''

''Almost three years ago now. Robin was in first grade, and at six years old, coming in contact with so many others her age, she was acutely conscious that while a few of her new school friends did not have a father at home, all of them but her had a mother. And they had the kind of mothers who baked cookies and cupcakes for Halloween and came to school to admire their children's work when it was displayed on the bulletin boards on parent's back-to-school night.''

''But you went to those events with her, I know. I remember one night during *Rowena's Daughter* that Corinne said you'd taken Robin to something at her school.''

''Sure I went. Audrey Rose even provided a good share of chocolate cupcakes with orange icing, but none of this made up in Robin's eyes for not having her mother there like the other kids did.'' He shrugged and continued. ''Well, now I've set the stage, I'll get to the action.'' He said this without glancing at Tori. She continued to watch him, noticing the slight frown that moved across his brow.

''Janet was home to spend Christmas with Robin. I give her credit for that. Robin begged her not to get a part in a play again for a long time, and the surprising thing was that Janet promised she would stay at home all winter.''

''That must have made Robin happy.''

Max nodded. ''Ecstatic is the word. And the thing that thrilled Robin the most was that Janet agreed to be the classroom mother in charge of their first grade Valentine's Day party. Robin was so excited she could hardly wait for February to get here, and she wore a constant smile on her face that I'll swear was as bright as brass in the sunshine.'' A dark look came over his face like a curtain and he said, ''That smile was destroyed three days before the scheduled party at Robin's school. And that was also the day that Robin got hurt.''

Tori saw the muscle working tensely in Max's jaw. She realized that it was not easy for him to tell her all of this. Unconsciously she rubbed one hand up and down her arm, anxious to learn about it, yet at the same time afraid she was going to regret hearing what Max would tell her.

''At nine o'clock that Saturday morning, Robin and I were still at the table having breakfast when Janet came in and made her fateful announcement. She was dressed in a suit, wearing her camel hair topcoat, and carrying two pieces of luggage. 'I'm leaving for Atlanta. I've got a part in a road company of *Will Rogers Follies,* and I've got a cab waiting downstairs to take me to the airport,' she said. Her words and manner showed her complete lack of concern as to what affect her actions would have on Robin. Well the scene that followed defies description. It was dreadful and even now it makes me sick all over to remember it.'' Max's voice rose in anger and he gripped the steering wheel so hard his knuckles whitened. ''I tried to reason with her. Begged her to think of Robin and at least wait until after the Valentine party to leave. Janet wouldn't listen to anything I said. She simply picked up her bags and went out the door. Robin ran after her, crying so hard she was almost hysterical. I grabbed Janet's arm as she headed for the taxi. 'If you leave now and do this to Robin, then don't bother to ever come back. Because frankly I won't care if I never see you again, and I doubt that Robin will care either.' I said that to her. I shouldn't have, and I didn't mean it. But I was just so angry, and at that moment I hated her for what she was doing to her own child.

''Janet didn't say anything, but she had the oddest expression on her face, and an almost wild look in her eyes. She swung away from me and flung open the door of the cab. Robin threw her arms around Janet's waist still crying and begging her not to go. Abruptly, Janet thrust Robin away, shoving her so hard that

Robin fell, hitting her head on the sharp edge of the open car door. That fall accounts for her scar.'' His tone was leaden.

Tears came springing to Tori's eyes. ''Oh Max,'' she exclaimed sadly, looking at him and seeing the lines of pain that wreathed his eyes and formed a network about his vulnerable mouth.

''There's more. The tragic repercussion came just three weeks later.''

''What do you mean?''

''That was the night Janet left the theater and stepped off the curb right in front of an oncoming firetruck with its siren blaring. She was killed instantly.''

Tori shuddered. ''I had no idea she died in such a tragic accident.''

''I'm not sure it was an accident.''

Tori scrutinized him, a shocked expression widening her eyes. ''How could it have been anything but an accident? No one in their right mind gets in the path of a racing firetruck.''

''Exactly,'' he said, a muscle clenching along his jaw. ''But after all that had happened with Robin, and what I'd shouted at her in my anger, who can guess what state of mind Janet might have been in. Particularly if she'd stopped taking her medication.''

''What sort of medication are you talking about?'' Tori was experiencing an assortment of confusing thoughts, and more than one question rose in her mind.

"Janet took daily doses of lithium to control those wide mood swings of hers. Without the medication she would experience periods of debilitating depression."

Suddenly it was as though a long-locked door had finally been opened to her, but only a crack, and Tori felt compelled now to open it wide. "Max, you can't possibly blame yourself for Janet's death."

"I'm not so sure I can't," he said gravely. "Except in the beginning I wasn't able to make her really happy. And I doubt that she truly loved anyone but Robin. So you see, when she left us that morning and I told her Robin wouldn't care if she never came back, I left Janet nothing to live for."

Tori laid her hand on Max's arm. "You're wrong to blame yourself for this. From what you've told me before about Janet's mood swings and her often erratic behavior, her problems stemmed from deeper, more complex things than you or Robin or anyone can understand. Maybe she wasn't always happy, but what happiness she knew you and Robin gave her. You should believe this and not conjure up some weird concept about Janet's death that has no basis whatsoever with the facts."

Max gave her an odd look. "You sound like Corinne. She told me that I should do as she does. Shut the past away, like something in a box with the lid tightly closed. She said that's the only way to live with it and not let it destroy you." His voice trailed away into a hoarse whisper.

The ribbon of road made a downhill descent, winding and coiling like a snake. Max coughed and cleared his throat. "We'd best talk about something else. Something more pleasant," he said after a long pause. "Don't you agree?"

"Yes," she nodded, looking at him, a hesitant smile on her lips.

He returned her look. They smiled at each other in a frightened way, like two people who have just said too much, and yet not quite enough.

Chapter Fourteen

The following morning at the rehearsal everyone gathered at the playhouse on time except for Lon. He was fifteen minutes late putting in an appearance. Dashing down the aisle and leaping up on the stage he apologized for holding things up. "I got a call from my agent just as I was leaving the lodge," he explained, his voice bright with excitement. He grabbed Tori around the shoulders. "I'm going to Kansas with Tori," he emphasized his words with a bear hug. "Jayson's signed me up for a part in the *Wheat Lands* miniseries."

Max shot Tori a look of surprise. "Well now, you hadn't told me about doing *Wheat Lands.*"

"I guess I forgot to mention it. I've only known about it for a couple of days."

''That's long enough to have told me.'' He scowled. ''Where do you film? And when?''

''In western Kansas, a place near Wichita. I have to be there the day after we finish the season here. Timing is going to be a bit tight.''

''Sounds like it,'' he muttered, glancing at his watch. ''Same with the rehearsal time for this play. Let's get started.'' He turned on his heels and walked off the stage.

Tori was conscious of the lisp of his leather shoes crossing the wooden stage, going away from her. Obviously Max was upset with her because she hadn't told him she was going to do the miniseries. But why? Did he expect her to discuss her acting plans with him. If so, he was going to have to tell her. She couldn't read his mind. And he hadn't indicated that he was particularly interested in what she planned to do after the summer ended. Her eyes grew unexpectedly moist. She'd begun to wonder if Max might phase her out of his life when they all left Summerville. If that was what he wanted then he should be relieved that she was making it easier for him by rushing off to Kansas. She raised her hand to her forehead hiding her eyes long enough to blink back the unwanted tears.

The sound of Max's shoes ceased. Tori opened her eyes and glanced out front to see him take an aisle seat on the third row. Immediately she moved to the center of the stage, taking her place for her opening lines.

Closing night of *Love Is a Soap Bubble*, Max invited the cast for a farewell party. They would all be off to different places the following day, and after the summer they'd shared they were all feeling sentimental at parting.

When their companionable banter took on a tinge of wistful nostagia Lon got to his feet. "Before you have me all teary-eyed let's break this up." He made a droll face.

"You would suggest that, just when I was ready to do the 'parting is such sweet sorrow' bit," Brandon countered with a sweeping gesture in which he took Corinne's hand and pulled her to her feet. "Come fairest lady of the theater, allow me to escort you to your room."

Max put a restraining hand over Tori's as the group broke up. "Don't you leave," he whispered under his breath. He entwined his fingers with hers, and her hand tingled pleasantly with the warmth of his touch.

"I wish you weren't going off to Kansas tomorrow with Lon," he said. "I hate the thought of not seeing you every day."

"You and Robin are going to Vermont, then back to New York. You'd not be seeing me anyway," she said, her voice like a faint thread of sound.

He shot her a perturbed look. "You're coming back

to New York after the *Wheat Lands* filming, aren't you?''

''If Jayson gets me an audition for a new play I might. I think he's more apt to get me another television offer. In which case I'll probably go to California.'' She managed to sound offhand about it, as if they were discussing her career moves and nothing personal.

''I want you in New York.''

''Do you?''

''You know darn well I do.'' He leaned his head closer to hers. ''Haven't I told you that I've grown accustomed to your face and the lovely way you walk?''

''You could watch me on television and see that,'' she answered without smiling.

Max examined her sober face, a frown shattering the warm light that had been in his caring eyes. ''Don't you want to be with me in New York? Is that it?'' he demanded, his eyes darkening now in anger. ''What the devil has gotten into you?'' he demanded in a steely voice.

Tori saw the hard contraction and release of his throat. But before she could speak he straightened his shoulders putting distance between them. ''It's that blasted miniseries and the incomparable Lon Taylor, isn't it?''

She was taken aback and stared at Max blankly, not comprehending at once what he was getting at.

"Well I certainly was a help to you there. Why, I paired you with Lon in *A Game of Musical Chairs,* a bit of casting brilliance on my part." His acid tone was caustic. "Making you have no further need of me professionally or personally. Right?"

She felt simultaneously hot and cold. Her dismay was because of the way Max was regarding her, with a sardonic expression that distorted his strong-boned face. "What are you saying?"

"You heard me," he snapped.

"I don't—can't understand you." She kept shaking her head in disbelief.

"Oh yes you can. You have Lon waiting in the wings now. A gifted young man without a wife in his past, and no guilt or regrets he needs to come to terms with either."

"Stop it!" Tori cried, her frustration with him turning to anger. "You're being absurd, and what you're saying is total nonsense."

"No, it isn't. Lon's feelings for you are certainly more than any casual friendship. You're not going to try to deny that."

"Lon is not an issue between you and me and never will be. So for heavens sake, quit suggesting that he is."

"If it's really not him, then what in the world is it?" He leaned closer again, lifting her chin with his hand to force her to look at him. "Darn it Tori, what we have going is special. It's good and right for both of us.'' He tempered his petulant tone, offering a slow smile of conciliation. ''I expect ours to be more than a summertime romance.''

''Yet not enough more that you'd risk your new play on it,'' she blurted without thinking. The second the revealing words flew out of her mouth she regretted them.

It was Max's turn to be taken aback. He stared at her, the picture of a man totally perplexed. ''How in creation did my new play get into this?''

''Forget it,'' she said quickly. ''I don't know why I said it.''

His eyes challenged hers. ''Yes you do. And I want to know what you mean.''

Tori felt the tightness across her shoulders increase until it was an ache all across her back. How should she handle this? Her mind raced, seeking an unemotional way to get around Max's question. Twist and turn as she did, she found none. ''There isn't time to go into it. It's so late,'' she said lamely.

''We'll make the time,'' he said tersely.

Tori pressed her lips together so tightly the color left them. She raised her chin, her eyes leveling unflinchingly on his. ''There's still a few people at the bar, Max. Let's not make an unpleasant scene out of this.'' Her voice shook and she was breathing erratically. Keeping her voice down, she said, ''I'm not altogether sure why I said what I did, Max. Call it a cheap shot. Maybe I just realized that you are more committed to the play you wrote than you can ever be to me.'' Saying this, she hesitated only a moment before she stood up and left the room.

Tori felt cold inside, cold and numb. Her words had struck a nerve with Max. There could be no doubt of that. He recognized the truth in what she'd said because he was not about to risk the long run of his new play on a relationship of questionable duration. For regardless of what he'd said about wanting more than a summer romance, if he believed they had a future together he would have produced *All the Tomorrows* here in Summerville with Corinne and her in the two leading women roles and then taken it on to Broadway.

Tori's tears came now, sliding unchecked down her cheeks as her heart hummed like a seashell with her pain-filled thoughts. When she reached the privacy of her own room, she closed the door firmly behind her, leaning against it, her head lowered, her arms clutched across her breasts as if shielding herself against further hurt.

That was the simple truth of it. Max had high expectations for *All the Tomorrows.* He anticipated a very long run for this his finest play. He'd told her that with the right cast it could go for three years or more. Apparently he neither planned nor hoped that what feelings he had for her would last that long.

If Max had viewed *All the Tomorrows* as just another play of his that would have one season on Broadway, it would be different. Max would desire and need her for one brief theater season, but he was afraid to commit himself to her for anything more. Tori knew that. She understood this about him far better than he understood it about himself. Tori saw the scars that his marriage had left. Scars that had to be erased, or at least healed, before he would risk making any real commitment to another woman. For what he'd been through with Janet had destroyed his confidence in his ability to give his love to a woman and know that the love he offered would make her happy and fulfilled.

Tori raised her head and moved away from the closed door. She hated the hopeless feelings she had. She was in love with Max. That wasn't going to change. Inside of her was the profound need for him to share himself and his life with her. That wasn't going to change either. He couldn't offer her this. And she could not accept less. Her eyes swam with tears. What a sad impasse she and Max had come to—immutably sad.

Tori didn't see Max alone again. Probably it was just as well. As it turned out it was a hassle getting away from Summerville by seven o'clock the next morning. She got to the airport in Albany with just minutes to spare before she and Lon boarded their flight to Chicago. In Chicago there would be a lengthy layover and a change of airlines before they could continue on to their destination in the center of the Kansas wheat belt.

For this reason Tori was grateful for Lon's affable company. She could not bear the thought of the long tedious trip by herself, being left to stare out the plane window into blue-white nothingness with just her unhappy thoughts for distraction.

In the close confines of the airplane, Tori and Lon had numerous hours to talk. They conversed about a wide assortment of things. When they appeared to run out of general subjects, Lon steered their conversation into more personal channels.

"I've got a favor to ask of you, Tori."

They had just taken off from Chicago on the second lap of the trip. Tori was gazing through the window as the plane gained altitude. She turned as Lon's words drew her attention away from the rapidly disappearing city beneath the jet.

"What kind of favor?" she asked.

"A big one. I want a claim on your free time while we're doing the miniseries."

She hunched her shoulders. "I doubt there'll be much of that."

"But will you spend what there is with me?" He looked at her with pleading eyes. "You see, you made my loneliness disappear while we were in Summerville. I don't want it to settle back down on me in Kansas."

"No chance. You may not realize it, but with the

large cast for *Wheat Lands,* plus the director, wardrobe people and television crew, we're talking scads of folks on this location. You'll find you're scarcely alone, believe me.'' She slanted her head toward him, giving a quick laugh.

''There's a difference between loneliness and being alone,'' he responded ruefully. ''Being alone is a choice of the mind, loneliness comes up through the heart and engulfs the spirit.''

''Hey, cut the melancholy lines. We're not doing Greek tragedy here.'' She made a wry face at him.

Lon frowned. ''Sorry. Sometimes I take myself too seriously, I guess.''

She knew from his voice that he felt rebuffed. She hadn't intended that. Lon was so intense and young. Tori remembered what Max had said about Lon's feelings for her. The thought made a gray shape in her mind. She did not want Lon waiting in the wings for her. It had been ridiculous for Max to say that she did.

''We all do that. It's no crime.'' She touched Lon's hand and smiled reassuringly. ''And until you run into some cute, young TV actress in the cast that you'll want to take up your time, what do you say we eat dinner together and run our lines for the next day's shooting?''

''That's what I wanted all along.'' A smile moved slowly on his mouth, easing the strained lines of his lean face. "Tori, you're good for me. You know that?"

She chuckled. "You make me sound like a natural grain cereal."

"One hundred percent whole wheat, ma'am," he drawled. "This is Kansas after all." He winked at her and they both laughed.

Chapter Fifteen

There are brief but lovely moments that come with autumn. Colors change swiftly. Leaves float to the ground like kites that lose the wind. Browns, yellows, crimsons, scarlets, the leaves ran the gamut of fall shades through these weeks Tori spent in Kansas.

On her last day of filming, the early sun of morning slanting from the east fell upon her back with comfortable warmth. The dying leaves of autumn made a warm, sweet odor in the Kansas air. Tori concentrated her thoughts on the color in the leaves, the muted browns and yellows that she liked. On this her last day in the easy-paced Kansas town, it was better to think back about her weeks here doing the miniseries than to speculate on what was ahead.

Her agent had called her several days ago about an

audition for a new Neil Simon play. It sounded good, but she had qualms about returning to New York. Those qualms were magnified later that day when she received an unexpected phone call.

"Max?" Tori's voice echoed her surprise at hearing from him. "How did you know where to get hold of me?"

"I asked Jayson. I was afraid you'd finished filming and might already have left Kansas."

"I'm leaving tomorrow."

"I know. That's what Jayson told me. Said you were coming here to audition for the Simon play. I'll meet your plane."

Stunned, since this was the last thing she could have imagined he would say, she was at a loss to answer.

"What time do you arrive? What's your flight number?" He cleared his throat nervously. "I have to see you tomorrow, Tori. Don't give me an argument."

"Who's arguing, Max?" she laughed. "It'll be nice to be met. Although isn't that a hassle for you?"

"You're worth a bigger hassle than that," he countered lightly. Then his voice sobered and he said. "I— I've got something rather unbelieveable to tell you when you get here." There was an element of suppressed excitement in the tone of his voice.

"Oh, what about?" she inquired curiously.

"Did you happen to read about that earthquake last week in Mexico?"

"Yeah, the pictures of Mexico City looked horrible. Several hundred killed or injured, weren't there?"

"Right, and the weird thing is that I've learned that earthquake affects me in an incredible way."

"You make it sound both interesting and mysterious."

"It's all that and more. It's a long story and it would take too long to make you understand on the phone. I'll tell you everything tomorrow. Say, will Lon be on the same plane with you?" he asked abruptly.

Max's veering the conversation to take in Lon struck a sour note with Tori. "No, he won't," she snapped. "He left here yesterday for Chicago. His parents live somewhere in Illinois and I think he's laying over a couple of days to see them." She didn't try to hide her irritation. "But you should know Lon's schedule, since he *is* coming to New York to be in your new play," she said caustically.

There was a noticeable moment of silence before Max said, "Lon told you I'd offered him the part of Corinne's son in *All the Tomorrows?*"

"Yes, he told me."

"That's something else I need to talk to you about when I see you."

"Scratch that subject, Max," she ordered. "There's no earthly reason for us to talk about Lon. And I certainly don't intend to."

"Hey, simmer down, darling. I didn't mean Lon. I meant the play." Max's throaty laugh sounded warm in her ear. "Meet you tomorrow," he said, then hung up without saying good-bye.

It took Tori a few seconds before his last words penetrated her mind. His play? What did Max want to say to her about that? Hadn't they argued enough over it already?

She nudged the phone aside and stretched out across the bed, lying on her stomach, her head resting on her crossed arms. What was Max trying to do? And how could that earthquake in Mexico City affect him? He had something important on his mind, but she couldn't figure out what it might be. He was so insistent about meeting her plane. The thought caused excitement to tingle through her. But then she came back to her senses. What a fool she was to love him like this. If she had an ounce of resolve, she'd cancel out on the audition for the Neil Simon play and tell Jayson to get her something to do on television out in California. She ought to put as much distance as possible between her and Max. For only distance and time could alter her feelings and lessen her need of him.

The short leg of Tori's flight from the Kansas town to St. Louis took less than an hour, but there was a layover before taking the connecting flight on east. This made her arrive in New York just at nightfall. The large aircraft descended through the starlit sky to meet the lights of the city rising like fireworks in the darkness.

Tori took her place in the stream of passengers filling the passageway that led from the plane into the terminal. As she emerged she saw Max waiting for her. She took in the rugged look of him, the dark eyes, the strong mouth faintly smiling. Her earlier qualms lifted like a fog as a treacherous warmth engulfed her.

When she came within his reach Max pulled her aside, hugging her to him, his strong arms secure around her. "I'm so glad you came back. All day I had an awful feeling that you'd change your mind and not come," he said, looking as if the sight of her elated him.

"I almost did. Because I thought it was a mistake to come back here."

"It's not a mistake. Believe me." He looked at her with a strange light dancing in his eyes. "Everything is different now. I'm different." He took his arms from around her, then catching hold of one of her hands he pulled her with him. "Let's get the heck away from here. Go somewhere I can tell you how really different I am. And why. . . . " He urged her quickly along in the direction of the luggage claim area.

By unspoken agreement they ceased personal comments in the taxicab heading into Manhattan. The taxi sped toward the city, darting from one lane to another, moving so fast that the view through the window was a blur of lights and indistinct forms. In record time they were making their way uptown among the other cars crowding on either side, tailgating and racing to make the lights. When the driver pulled to a stop in front of Max's apartment, Tori looked surprised. "I thought we'd drop off my luggage at my place."

Max leaned forward handing several bills to the driver. "We'll do that later," he said, climbing from the cab and helping Tori out. "Audrey Rose made dinner for us here. One of her outstanding casseroles. You don't mind eating in do you?" he asked as he carried her luggage and they entered the elevator.

"Of course not. Sounds great to me and I'll get to see Robin."

"Later you can. But dinner is just the two of us. Audrey Rose took Robin for pizza and a movie. You see I wanted you and I to be alone so we could talk." His eyes held hers as he said this. There was no one else in the elevator with them so Max drew her into arms, lowering his face close to hers. Tori closed her eys and the next moment felt the soft touch of his lips on hers. Her arms moved up around his neck. Max pressed her closer in response. His mouth grew firmer and it was more than a kiss. It was a searching, seeking, hungry touching. Tori responded instinctively with a kind of desperation mingled with fierce joy.

The elevator rose to Max's floor and stopped. He relaxed his hold on her as the elevator doors slid quietly open. Tori felt dazed and breathless. She held on to Max afraid he'd let go of her entirely, but his arms stayed around her waist. For a meaningful moment his dark eyes probed hers, then his mouth twitched in a smile. "I should live on the top floor. I'd find it exciting to climb higher with you in my arms."

Warmth rushed into her cheeks. "We've gone far enough. I find I'm dizzy at this altitude," she teased him, laughing and pushing him gently away. Bending over she picked up the smaller of her two pieces of luggage and stepped off the elevator.

Max unlocked the door to his apartment and walked in ahead of Tori, flipping light switches to illuminate the inviting interior of his spacious apartment. Tori uttered an exclamation of approval as her eyes took in the well-arranged living area. It embodied traditional American comfort with the added appeal of subtle Oriental accents. The partially vaulted ceiling, coupled with floor to ceiling windows, gave an illusion of space that balanced a generous amount of furniture and kept it from overpowering the setting.

Max took a minute to place her luggage behind the planter in the entry hall where it was shielded from view by an artful oriental tree.

"This is a lovely, comfortable room," Tori said when he joined her. "I like everything about it," she added as she walked to the coffee table and bent over to admire an arrangement of yellow carnations in a blue cloisonné bowl. "Hmm, beautiful flowers," she murmured.

"They're for you. You told me once that yellow flowers were your favorite."

"You remembered that?" She turned to him, beaming with pleasure. "You're wonderful."

"I know." He grinned.

"You're also up to something and you're making me nervous. All that hinting at mysterious changes and saying things are different. For heaven's sake. When are you going to explain whatever it is?" She sat down on the sofa, indicating she wanted him to sit beside her.

"Okay. Just let me get us a soda first."

Max walked to the opposite side of the room where two Chinese screens slid apart to reveal a recessed bar. Tori felt too warm, so she got up and took off the navy blue blazer she'd worn on the plane, folding it over the back of the nearest chair. Before taking her seat again, she smoothed the sides of her trim, belted skirt and adjusted the cuffs of her white silk blouse. None of this was necessary, but it occupied her hands and stilled her impatience until Max returned.

"You're going to be really surprised by what I'm going to tell you. It certainly blew my mind," he said, handing Tori her drink, then sitting down next to her. She slanted her head at him attentively and waited for him to go ahead with it. "It happened a few days after that earthquake in Mexico City. Corinne came to me with a story out of her past that has far reaching ramifications, believe me." He paused long enough to take a swallow of his drink. "Didn't you ever wonder why Corinne never had married Griff?"

"Sure, I thought about it, I guess. But it was their business, and I figured she had her reasons."

"She did. Legal reasons. She was never divorced from the actor she married when she was eighteen."

Tori's eyes widened in astonishment. "Wow! That's really something. So, who is he? Where is he?"

"His name was Kent Sadler. He was killed in that earthquake in Mexico City. She got official notification from the Red Cross. And it was because he's now dead that Corinne was willing to finally tell me."

"Are you saying that Corinne stayed married to this Kent somebody all these years without anybody knowing it?"

"Yeah, she never told anyone but Griff, of course. It was her way of insuring that the mistakes she'd made would be kept secret. She had reasons to bury her past, and she went to extremes to do it."

"What reasons could call for anything that drastic?"

"I'll tell you just the way Corinne told me. Then you'll see."

Tori surmised she was in for a long story. She relaxed against the sofa cushions, taking sips of her soda. Max sat forward, angling his body so he could look at her. "It seems Corinne and this Kent Sadler were acting together in an off-Broadway play of some kind when they fell in love. She married him without knowing much of anything about him."

"That doesn't sound like Corinne," Tori quipped.

"You're forgetting that she was barely eighteen, and she'd come to New York from a small provincial town in New Hampshire. A savvy guy who'd worked some of the clubs and had bit parts in a couple of shows swept her off her feet. She married him for better or for worse, that's all."

"Obviously you're going to tell me it was for worse."

Max frowned and she detected a nerve jerking along the edge of his jaw. "Well, she certainly didn't pick a winner. Corinne told me that marrying Kent was the biggest mistake of her life."

"She must have thought she was in love with him though. Don't you think?"

Max was still frowning. "Probably in the beginning. She got over it fast however. Seems this fellow had a two-sided personality, one bright, one dark. Apparently he had an explosive temper and an abusive attitude."

Shocked to hear this, Tori asked. "Are you saying he physically abused Corinne?"

"She didn't say that. Yet from what she did tell me I'd believe he could have. At any rate he evidently had fits of temper directed at other actors and a director or two. After a while he couldn't even get any acting jobs."

"That's a bleak picture if I ever heard one."

"It gets worse," Max said gravely. "He and Corinne had been married close to two years by this time, and Kent was taking his failure and frustrations out on her. Corinne told me she hated to come home from the theater at night, as most of the time he was in some black, despairing mood.''

''He sounds paranoid to me.''

Max nodded, agreeing with her. ''That's why it was a relief to Corinne to come home after a performance one night and discover that Kent had packed up and taken off.''

''He walked out and left her?'' Her voice rose in disbelief.

''Yeah. And before he went he checked every bit of money they had out of the bank.''

''That was a scummy trick.''

''I'd say so. Particularly since most of it was money Corinne had made. She was the only one with an acting job at this point.''

''What a no-good leech he was,'' Tori said derisively. ''Did he have the decency to tell her where he was going?''

''He left a note saying he was leaving to go find a job someplace away from New York. Said when he did, he'd let her know.''

''Did he?''

''No, he sure didn't.''

Tori rotated her wine glass, swirling the liquid and regarding it absently. ''Good grief, Max. If they'd only been married two years then Corinne couldn't have been more than twenty when this happened.''

"That's right. She was really just getting a real toe hold on her career."

"So why didn't she get herself a smart lawyer and get free of this loser. After all, he took their money and ran out on her. Surely that constitutes desertion."

"Probably. I don't know. Remember though, she didn't know where he'd gone, had no money to spend tracking him down." He paused and cupped his chin in his hand. "Besides, now there were extenuating circumstances."

She eyed him over the rim of her glass. "Like what?" she asked.

"Like Corinne finding out she was pregnant."

Tori stared at Max aghast. It wasn't possible. Corinne had never had a baby, Tori reflected. She couldn't have kept that a secret. If she'd ever given birth to a child the whole world would know it. After all, she was a famous actress and every part of her life now or in the past was newsworthy. Tori's mind whirled crazily. All these sad details from Corinne's past. What did they have to do with Max anyway? Why was he so insistent to tell her what she could only think Corinne had told him in confidence?

"I'm not sure Corinne would want you telling me any of this," she said finally, coming out of her jumbled thoughts.

"I don't give a darn what Corinne wants," he said, rising to his feet and carrying his empty glass to the bar. "For a long time she played games with other peoples lives, mine included. Now she's finally owned up to the havoc she created. I've earned the right to tell you, and everybody else who needs to know, exactly what she told me.'' His voice rose in anger.

''Okay.'' She stood up, quickly crossing the room to join him. ''Don't get so worked up about it. You've got me terribly curious. So tell me.''

Placing ice cubes in his glass, Max fixed himself another drink before he continued. ''At the time her husband left her, Corinne had a part in a play that had ten more weeks to run. It wasn't difficult for her to manage that without anyone discovering her condition. The day after the play closed she slipped off to her sister's home in New Hampshire. She stayed there until her baby was born.''

''I know you're going to tell me something sad,'' she interrupted him, a look of compassion in her eyes. ''Corinne gave her child up, didn't she?''

Max nodded. ''Corinne was ever prudent, and her older sister and her husband were childless. It was inevitable that they should take Corinne's baby girl.'' He related this matter-of-factly, but the shimmer in his eyes as he looked directly at Tori belied his unemotional tone.''

Comprehending the full significance of what Max had just said, Tori's face blanched with shock. ''Janet,'' she breathed, scarcely moving her lips.

He nodded again. ''That's right. My wife was Corinne's daughter. I was as shocked as you are when she admitted this to me.''

''Janet was never told—even after she was a grown woman.''

''No. Corinne and her sister had a sworn agreement that she was never to know she was adopted. Then if she turned out to look like Corinne, it would only be natural for a girl to resemble her mother's sister.'' His lips twisted wryly. ''Our Corinne thought of every contingency.''

Tori still held her soda glass tightly clutched in her chilled hand. She set it down on the bar and rubbed her palms together. ''You never showed me a picture of Janet. Did she look like Corinne?''

He shook his head. ''Evidently she took after Kent. It's Robin who got Corinne's auburn hair.''

''I hadn't thought about Robin.'' She blew a sigh through her lips. ''You are going to have to tell her this, aren't you?''

''You can help me do that when the time is right,'' he said quietly.

Tori caught her breath sharply, turning her head to escape his gaze. ''It's a family matter. I think Corinne might want to help you.''

''There's more to Corinne's story,'' he said.

Tori walked away from the bar. She took a seat again on the sofa. Max followed her but did not take a seat. Rather he stood, leaning one shoulder against the edge of the marble fireplace. ''Corinne believes that Janet learned she was adopted.''

''But who would have told her?''

''Well, it seems her sister's husband never agreed with keeping the truth from Janet. He felt they ran the risk of her finding out some other way, and this would surely make her suspicious about her real parentage.''

''Then Corinne thinks he told her.''

''She thinks when he knew he was dying that he did, yes. You see Janet was about fourteen then. Corinne says it was about that time that Janet's attitude toward her changed, became less open. A few years later when Janet was ready for college she wanted to attend Columbia and be in New York. This surprised Corinne. She found it odd that Janet suddenly chose to be where she was. It was the beginning of Janet's love-hate attitude toward Corinne.''

Tori looked bemused. ''Do you think her ambivalence was as strong as that?''

''It could have been if she saw Corinne as a totally self-centered woman who never loved nor wanted her own daughter,'' he said ruefully.

''Do you believe Janet saw Corinne that way?'' she asked, studying Max's intelligent face with questioning eyes.

''Yes, I do. After hearing Corinne's theory, I have no reason to argue with it,'' he answered with quiet but firm resoluteness.

''And this theory is what exactly?''

"That Janet felt a malice toward Corinne that was a basis for everything she did—her strange behavior— her almost frantic need to be constantly on tour with one roadshow after another—and her spells of depression—ultimately even her reckless and self-destructive carelessness that led to her death."

"Oh, Max," Tori shuddered, shaking her head sadly. "That's a horrible picture of Janet's life."

He nodded. "I know. But it's plausible, and even understandable, considering she was Kent's daughter too. She inherited his dark side, his uneven personality and erratic behavior." Max's expression was morose. "This is Corinne's theory I've been telling you, but heaven knows I've seen for myself some of the strange twists Janet's ambivalent thinking could take."

"Tell me about that," she prodded him.

"Take for instance, the fact that she refused to go to a single one of Corinne's performances. Yet, she wanted me to write plays for Corinne and direct her in them." Max ran his hand inside his collar and rubbed the back of his neck. "I know it sounds bizarre, but now I wonder if this may have been Janet's way to take revenge."

Tori frowned at him. "I don't follow that."

He angled his head and made a wry grimace. "Corinne was able to reject her own daughter, but she'd never be able to reject her daughter's husband. Not as long as he created her greatest success for her. Sounds crazy but that's the way Janet looked at it. And she took satisfaction from it apparently.'' Max gave a humorless laugh. ''Think about this point too. Janet's wanting to have a baby was motivated by her wanting to prove she could be the caring, nurturing mother Corinne had never been.''

''You know, in a way, I think I can understand why Janet would want to make Corinne suffer feelings of guilt over what she did. And maybe she has. Who knows?''

''Who indeed,'' Max said, stiffening his shoulders and setting his empty glass on the mantle. ''I only thank the powers that be that Corinne finally felt compelled to tell me the truth about Janet. Understanding this has made it possible for me to put everything in perspective.'' He ran his hand along the polished edge of the marble mantle. ''Now I want to make you see the difference this has made in my thinking, in fact in every aspect of my life.'' He stepped away from the fireplace and came over to where she sat. ''At last I can put the past behind me. I need you though, Tori, to help me carry out all my plans for the future.''

Max sat down on the sofa beside her, taking Tori's glass and placing it on the coffee table. Then he took her hand, raised it to his lips and kissed her cool finger tips.

This sudden bit of tender affection from Max heated more than just her fingers. She felt as if warm air were closing over her like a sauna. ''Wh—what sort of help?'' she asked tentatively.

"I've three things to ask you," he said quietly, pressing her hand now firmly in his. His eyes on hers were anxious, questioning. "I want you to take the part in my new play."

Drawing back in surprise, Tori studied him intently without answering. As if he read her unspoken thoughts he added, "I'm in dead earnest about this. I want you in *All the Tomorrows* with Corinne and Lon."

"You mean be in the original cast and play this first season?"

"I mean this opening season and all that follow. It's your role Tori for the entire run of the play." He looked at her with such a caring smile that it caused her heart to stir very stealthily and turn over.

"Before I answer, I'd like to hear the other two things you want to ask."

"That's only fair, I guess." He inched closer, and letting go of her hand he gently laid his palm against her cheek. "I'm really asking this for Robin. Because it's something she said she wants you, and only you, to do for her."

"What's that?"

"She told me to tell you that she'd like it *awfully much* if you'd be the one to take her to have her hair styled with bangs that would hide her scar. And if you think it's all right she'd like to have enough curl put in her hair to make it curve up in the back like a duck's behind. Her words, not mine." He laughed.

Tori's face was wreathed with her pleased smile. "I'd truly love to do that with Robin. I'm happy that she would ask for me."

"She likes you. In fact, you're special to her. You're special to me too," he said, tracing her cheeks with his fingertips. A second later he tenderly followed the angles of her jaw and chin and gently tipped her face up to his. "I remember that you said I was more committed to my play than I'd ever be to you. But that's not true." Max spoke in a firm, even tone and his eyes didn't waver as they gazed steadily into hers. "I now have a greater commitment I want to make to you."

All of a sudden sparks of hope danced through Tori's mind, spreading excitement through her. When Max pulled her to him in a tight embrace, her eyes were shimmering with tears of happiness. She buried her face in his shoulder as he hugged her close.

They simply held each other for several hushed minutes. Finally Max's lips found hers and they kissed deeply and for a long time, needing the physical oneness that wiped out the last shreds of doubt as a clean flame cuts through cobwebs.

Max was the one to break them apart. As he eased his head away slightly, he rubbed her cheek with his. "Before we get completely carried away darling, don't you want to know the third thing?" his voice was teasing. "You do know I'm talking lasting commitment here. I want you to marry me, Tori."

Happiness put the sound of joyous laughter into her voice as she quipped. "You'd go to such lengths as marriage to get me to take that role in your play?"

"You bet your life I would," he said, looking at her through eyes narrowed with desire. "You better understand this right here and right now. I've absolutely no intention of facing *all the tomorrows* without you!"

Tori laughed, elation soaring inside her. "Well, that sounds like a guaranteed run of the play contract to me."

"Try run of our lives contract—time without end," Max said, pulling her close again.

She settled into the secure haven of his arms with a contented sigh. "Time without end. That's beautiful, Max. You must use that in a play sometime."